PASSING THROUGH
THE MAJESTIC:

TALES OF MAGICAL SUMMERS INSPIRED
BY CRYSTAL BEACH

*Dearest Renata —
With much
love — Arlynne S. Braun*

Arlynne S. Braun

PASSING THROUGH THE MAJESTIC: TALES OF MAGICAL
SUMMERS INSPIRED BY CRYSTAL BEACH/ Braun 1st Edition

ISBN: 978-1-953610-52-2

　　　1. Short Stories Collection
　　　2. Fiction>Short Stories
　　　3. Regional> Western New York
　　　4. Regional> South-East Canada
　　　5. Regional> Crystal Beach
　　　6. Female Authors

Illustrations done by Dorothy Bevan

NFB
<<<>>>
NFB Publishing/Amelia Press
119 Dorchester Road
Buffalo, New York 14213

For more information visit
Nfbpublishing.com

For Irv, who gave me wings to fly.

FOREWORD

My sisters and I grew up spending summers at our grandparents' cottage, the Majestic, where the wind seemed to dance through every space in the house as if it were an open-air playground, bringing the fresh water smell of the great Lake Erie just a block away. One didn't even have to walk to the beach to smell the coconut suntan lotion and breathe in the aroma of French fries and vinegar. Whether the sun shone or not, the stall on the beach would be crowded with hungry vacationers jostling their slick arms to vie for vanilla ice cream cones-- the vanilla not scooped but cut off as a rectangle and placed securely on the crispy cone. As children, we always felt safe and secure; there would always be the wind, the lake, and the cottage.

Mom put down her pen while raising us daughters, and when she picked it up again in 2016, stories of the Majestic in Crystal Beach, Ontario, just across Lake Erie from Buffalo, flowed out. Arlynne Braun has never forgotten the sight and smells that influenced her childhood. What a privilege it has been to read these stories and get reacquainted with lost relatives, friends and places. I invite you to share in the journey that Lori, Julie and I were so fortunate to be a part of.

Susan Braun Svorai

May 2022

AUTHOR'S NOTE

I would like to thank my three remarkable daughters for all their love and help in the creation of this book. Two live far away but my youngest, Julie is nearby. When she'd visit, there would always, accidentally on purpose, be a copy of my newest story lying around and she would always pick it up and read it, usually with a smile on her face.

My eldest daughter Lori, lives in Florida, and regularly received my stories by email, whether she wanted to or not. On her visits here, one of our nightly rituals involved me reading her my tales as she snuggled in bed at night, ready for sleep, so similar to how I read her children's stories as a child.

Susan, my middle daughter, lives abroad. Sue is an English teacher and has been most instrumental in helping me get this book finished, acting as my coach and editor. Although a stern taskmaster, she lovingly guided me through this journey, and I thank her for her relentless persistence and encouragement.

I want to acknowledge my sister Linda and my niece Amy for all their loving support.

Lastly, I want to thank my sister, Myrna, who suffered through countless readings over the telephone during the worst days of the pandemic with endless patience.

In retrospect, I really don't know if I would ever have been able to finish *Passing Through the Majestic*, if not for the pandemic's forced isolation.

Suddenly I had the time.

Contents

1

The Majestic Becomes Majestic

It was a pivotal moment when my mother and card playing friend Tilly decided to rent a cottage together at Crystal Beach, Ontario, for the entire summer, particularly because they had never gotten along exceptionally well.

The bleached wood rental they chose was within walking distance of Hall's Crystal Beach Amusement Park and the Lake Erie beach and a short boat ride or car trip from our year-round home in Buffalo. There were four bedrooms to be divided among us. Besides our parents, I had a sister Myrna, two years younger than me and an eighteen-month-old baby sister, Linda. Tilly was a young widow and mother of two rambunctious boys. These larger, older boys seemed especially rough and tough but then again, we were accustomed to only girls in our family.

As there was no postal service in our small village, addresses were of little use, so residents gave their summer homes names to differentiate them. Optimistically, Dad christened our cottage "Serenity" but, in reality, it was never serene. It should have been dubbed "Chaos," but we didn't know it at that time.

Everything went well at the cottage for a while as both women tried to muddle through despite their ingrained differences. However, it was inevitable right from the beginning that these two were not going to exist peacefully for very long. Tilly was a lighthearted woman who did not take well to her friend's more structured style of living. Mother was a planner; she made lists and was adamant about having orderliness in her life.

Mother viewed Tilly's rowdy boys with disdain. She felt they had been brought up without boundaries or good manners. "Tilly lets them get away with being rude and sloppy," she intoned. "They think the world revolves around them." Dad said nothing but nodded nervously.

The truth of the situation was that no one could imagine Tilly behaving any differently than she did. Tilly was a fun-loving, flighty woman who simply wasn't overly concerned with the minutiae of everyday living. Tilly never gave a thought to dinner preparations until supper time rolled around. She'd make peanut butter sandwiches for her boys and call it a feast. Her sons didn't care because they were happily spread out on a beach blanket, watching the sun go down as they ate their supper. All the many things we liked about Tilly—her humor, spontaneity, her childlike ways—our mother simply couldn't abide.

One morning Tilly came up with what she thought was a grand idea. She felt she could make do with one bedroom and suggested subletting her second in order to earn some extra money. My parents were opposed. They disliked the thought of having strangers around, especially as there was only one bathroom already shared by eight people.

"What about the kitchen, parlor, and porch we all use?" Mother's voice rose. "Everything here doesn't just belong to you to do with as you choose, even if you're happy to all live in one room, using sleeping bags, yet."

Tilly snapped back, "There are five people in your family. Mine only has three. I've split all expenses with you even-steven and didn't complain. Why shouldn't I rent out my second bedroom if I want to earn some extra cash? Who are you to stop me?"

Dad said, "You know this was never part of the deal."

Tilly revisited this proposal daily, and daily my mother trampled it. My mother was a pretty woman, dark haired, green eyed, petite. Because of her sweet face, she could be mistaken for someone soft and pliable, but beneath that guise was a lioness of a woman and no way was Tilly a match for her grit. If our mother did not agree to her friend's desire to sublet that extra room, there was no way it was ever going to happen, no matter how vigorously or how often Tilly pled.

One morning after another discussion on this old familiar topic, Mother mumbled so softly we weren't sure we'd heard right. "It just might work out if you split whatever you make from that room right down the middle." While Dad was astonished to hear those words come out of his wife's mouth, he was secretly delighted that these two women might be nearing a path to a compromise.

After a great deal of wrangling, Mother agreed that Tilly could keep sixty percent of any rent collected and she would get forty percent. However equitable this might seem to an outsider, the terms never sat well with either of them as both were sure they were getting the short end of the stick.

Our new tenants were a pleasant older couple who barely made a ripple in our everyday life. Although this segment of their arrangement had worked out better than anyone could have possibly imagined, other elements of their living together had worsened. Mother was constantly annoyed with Tilly. "I will never, ever share a cottage with Tilly again," she vowed to my dad. "I'm always cleaning up after her boys. They drag sand in every time they walk through the cottage, drop wet towels all over the place and leave their dirty dishes everywhere. Tilly does nothing to correct them. She says, 'They're just kids,' like that makes everything okay."

Dad, desperately searching for a happy resolution when it came to keeping peace between the two of them, put his arm around his wife. "Hey, Sweetheart, this is only a place to lay our heads. It's only because we decided to split the costs with Tilly that we're able to stay here the entire summer," he reminded her.

She continued as if he had not spoken. "Worst of all is that the toilet seat is always up! In the middle of the night, I went to the bathroom and fell into the toilet! God forbid Tilly should ever correct her crown princes. Instead, she has the nerve to say to me, 'Let's just keep the lid up all the time.' Like that's a solution? I put a note near the toilet to remind them to put that seat down" she declared, "and I underlined the word DOWN."

"Your wife thinks she's the boss of me. Clean this! Clean that! Pick up this! Pick up that!" Tilly groused to Dad. "She's way too fussy! Such a dictator! So what if one of my kids forgets about the toilet seat or leaves a towel on the floor? It's not the end of the world. Boys just don't think about things like that. I think it's little enough to put up with when it's my room bringing in extra cash without any help from her royal highness," she grumbled. Dad sighed.

Despite their constant griping, Mother and Tilly soldiered on during that long, hot summer. While happy to have escaped the heat of the city, they were both anxious for their time together to end, now that it was the end of August. Mother and Tilly still felt there was great inequality regarding the revenue split, although the outcome resulted in each having extra dollars in their pockets with minimal effort. They had done quite a bit better than expected as that room was always occupied. This undeniable truth sparked Mother's ingenuity. If she were to own, rather than rent, a larger cottage with extra bedrooms to let, it could be a great moneymaker.

By the end of that summer, our parents made the momentous decision to seek out a property in Crystal Beach to buy. This would allow them to enjoy a free vacation and some extra income without bubble-headed Tilly and her progeny.

Thoughts of days at the shore dim from people's consciousness by the time fall arrives, but not so for my mother and father. They had become obsessed with acquiring a property in Crystal Beach before the next summer. Off they would trek from Buffalo every weekend to that stark, isolated village throughout the iciest months of winter, searching for a place with a few extra bedrooms that was within walking distance to the lake. It had to be in decent condition and affordable, so it couldn't be too large.

In the bitter month of February, 1950, their quest ended. The cottage was more expensive than they had planned but also considerably bigger. Their prize was blanketed in mounds of snow, windows frosted from the cold, and garnished with icicles hanging from the eaves. Located on a large lot, it had six guest rooms, living space for our family, plus two wood cabins in the back. As soon as they saw it, they knew this was the one they wanted, even though it wasn't what they had envisioned. Quickly, they put in a ridiculously low bid, and just as quickly it was accepted.

My parents, Ida and Harry, were now the proud owners of a grand two-story whitewashed cottage/boarding house with a wraparound porch and a substantial mortgage. They were overwhelmed, frightened, exhilarated. "What have we done?" Dad gasped as he and Mom danced about the kitchen with glee.

There was never any question about what to name their establishment. Even though it never remotely lived up to its haughty moniker, it became "The Majestic" forevermore.

2
My Summer Home

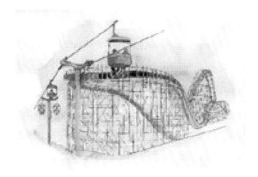

The sale on the boardinghouse cottage closed at the end of March, 1950. On a chilly day shortly after, we crossed the international border from the United States to Canada to see just what our parents had bought in Crystal Beach, Ontario. The first time I saw the Majestic, I was awed by its size—at least twice that of our two-family home in Buffalo. Our mission that day was to assess what needed doing, which was probably a lot. The Majestic had been unoccupied for a year and a half at least.

The first thing I saw when I walked into the Majestic was my own reflection caught in a full-length antique mirror encased in a gilded frame. It was mounted on the wall directly facing the doorway as if it were personally welcoming me to come inside. This magnificent art deco piece from the 1920s was much too grand for a summer home, but since Crystal Beach had been established as a village in 1888, so many items in cottages were reminders of times long past.

Fortunately, the Majestic had been built for year-round living and had a gas furnace that warmed everything quickly almost as soon as Dad lit the pilot light. Unfortunately, that was our mother's cue to open every window in the place to let in cold, fresh air. Unless you were directly in the parlor where the furnace was, the warmth was minimal.

Dad groaned, "What was the purpose of me turning the furnace on?"

The white clapboard cupboards in the main kitchen were filled with an abundance of dishes, glasses and bowls in need of washing, sitting on shelves that needed washing themselves. This job was assigned to my sister Myrna and me. Once we removed the multitude of items stored on these shelves, the undertaking seemed insurmountable. We stacked things everywhere, on the table, stove, chairs, floor.

Our fussy mother carefully examined all the items we had brought out from the deep recesses of these cabinets, and anything even slightly chipped, cracked or discolored was immediately tossed into the trash bin. She would never abide such items any place she lived in even if it were only for a few short months out of the year.

Amongst this hodgepodge we discovered an English teapot sprinkled with rose buds and earthenware coffee mugs. When my finger flicked the delicate crystal wine glasses, the goblet trilled. Mismatched sets of fine China lay alongside heavy beer steins, glazed serving bowls, oriental vases, Depression glass, and milky, hobnailed plates. These items all shared the same space. How had so much even fit in those cupboards?

Little did my sister or I know nor care that we were scouring antiques with careless abandon. All that mattered to us was getting that eclectic collection washed, dried and sorted back where it had so long been collecting dust.

Once the weather got better, I was able to appreciate the Majestic more, especially its large veranda. White-washed, wicker furniture brought out of storage lent it grace and a kind of gentility. Wind chimes hanging from the eaves whispered to us even on the calmest of days. By then the wild shrubbery that surrounded the exterior of the Majestic was tamed by Dad, and molded into vibrant green borders. Spring flowers—daffodils, irises, tulips—planted so many years ago, broke through the soil. Rose bushes bloomed.

Each time we came, there was less work to do and more to enjoy. By the end of May, the Majestic was completely functional. The nearby Hall's Crystal Beach Amusement Park opened on Memorial Day and immediately everything wondrously changed.

Suddenly there was a special place to go. It beckoned with tantalizing aromas of lemon, butterscotch, peanut and cinnamon, even from afar. At the entrance to the park stood a concession stand creating delicious hard candy suckers on site. These treats were so large, they could never be called lollipops. There was no other place to purchase this special treat except at that particular stand.

In the near center of the park loomed a twenty-foot statue of Paul

Bunyan. He looked like an endearing spirit, erected there to watch over us all. Past the statue, down a concrete walkway was the entrance to miles and miles of sandy beaches. The Pirate Ship ride, with black Jolly Roger flags, was close by and afforded a panoramic view of that part of the park and lake as it swung to and fro, higher and higher. It gave me pause to think that should there be a flaw in the machinery, I could drop like a rock into the shallowest part of the lake.

Elsewhere, the amusements were tamer. There was the Caterpillar ride that simply went round in circles. When its green canopy shell rolled down, skittish riders would squeal because suddenly it was pitch dark inside. Among my favorites was Laff in the Dark, a spooky ride where ghosts and monsters randomly appeared, supposedly to terrify, but were instead a laugh in the dark. I also loved the Magic Carpet ride, a funhouse full of surprises.

The *S.S. Canadiana* ferried its first load of passengers from Buffalo to Crystal Beach about eleven o'clock each morning. The vessel could transport three thousand people over in one sailing and made six round trips daily. Once the passengers disembarked, there was an electricity in the air that hadn't been there moments before. Our sleepy little village awakened; important visitors had landed.

Many folks headed directly to the grove for lunch and then onto the beach. It was a distance of at least one-half mile before the waters became deep enough to swim in. Soft mounds of sand cushioned your feet and seaweed tickled your toes as you made your journey into the deeper part of the lake, far past toddlers building sandcastles near the shore.

The park was peppered with red wooden booths where cash could be exchanged for tickets. These tickets were not only intended for rides but could also be used at food concessions that emitted the delicious smells of charred meats, powdered sugar waffles, French fries doused in vinegar, freshly popped popcorn dripping with butter and cinnamon apples on a stick. By late afternoon, the midway was swarming with hordes of people.

Pony rides for little kids were located furthest away from that noisy area. The pastoral scene of small children riding gentle ponies accompanied by farm boy escorts was skewed by the unexpected infusion of colorful gypsy tents spread out on the grass. Parents could get their fortunes told for twenty-five cents as their children rode the tiny horses. It was an interesting pairing.

A diminutive locomotive with cushioned seats and a canvas canopy was a favorite ride. With great fanfare, the conductor would announce, "The train is leaving the station." A parting bell sounded its departure, and the little locomotive would chug past bigger and brighter amusement rides, skim the border of our village streets, and then adventurously plunge into the woods surrounding the park property. It was always an exciting trip, albeit never long enough.

There was no admission charge to enter the park. Even if I didn't have the tickets needed for amusements, there was always something to do in the grove. Within the area lay a heavily shaded picnic site outfitted with wood picnic tables and steel grills laid over stone pits not far from a fully equipped playground

The most unusual aspect of the grove was that in its midst lived a pair of exotic peacocks encased in a wrought iron, oriental cage.

The male peacock would strut about, arrogantly displaying his magnificent plumage to a spellbound audience. Many of us had never seen a peacock. It saddened me that such regal birds lived in so humble an abode.

At night, everything in the park was brilliantly lit, a massive kaleidoscope of colors that twinkled and sparkled. The calliope played old familiar melodies as the carousel spun round and round on its circular orbit. Mirrored surfaces on the ride caught quick flashes of joyful people riding the magnificent beasts of the carousel that were at once realistic, yet incredibly mystical.

In 1924 an elegant dance hall called the Crystal Ballroom had been built close to the water's shore. Its rear doors swung wide onto a balcony that overlooked Lake Erie. Reflections from the multi-colored lights of the attractions would shimmer and shine on the waves below as music burst forth from the many popular bands that played there. People twirled beneath a revolving crystal ball as pinpoints of light sprinkled down upon them. Unconstrained, the music erupted from the dance hall, poured out onto the midway and echoed throughout the park.

When I was a child, I dwelt in a large white cottage of many, many rooms filled with many, many people. Every day, I watched the magnificent *Canadiana*, so resembling a many-tiered wedding cake, glide to and fro over the waves. The waters I swam in were tranquil and the sand glistened with crystal chips. For a quarter I could get my fortune told and for no cost at all, I could visit the resplendent peacocks that made their home in the grove.

3
First Year

The first year we were at the Majestic was the very best one for my sister and me because the cottage was operating below capacity. Our boarding house wasn't that well known yet, and there always were some vacancies.

That season, I always had my own bedroom at least until someone wanted to rent it, and then I'd cheerfully move into an empty one. I was extremely happy my parents had bought the Majestic for this reason alone. I didn't have to share a room with Myrna.

I loved my sister Myrna dearly, but I didn't like living with her. Our bedroom in the city wasn't that large and with the twin beds in our room at home in Buffalo it also felt overcrowded I inherited my mother's neatness gene and constantly quarreled with Myrna over the messy condition we coexisted in. Dad attached a white rope that hung taut right down the center of our room to separate our limited space. It was only minimally successful as Myrna used the rope as a clothesline to hang her belongings.

In the mornings, my sister and I would rush through our chores in the cottage and then put Linda in her stroller for some fun time in the park's playground. We could never stay as long as Linda would have liked because there were always errands to be done. First, we'd stop at a grocery store for basics like milk and eggs. From there we might head over to a bakery for bread or to the butcher's for hamburger or visit a fruit and vegetable stand for berries. There were no large food markets where everything could be bought in one place, so there were many quick stops we'd have to make. Regardless, by noon our errands were done, and we were ready to head out to the beach for the day.

Mother would leave with Linda shortly after we did, to spend her afternoon with her friends in the grove or on the shore. Ordinarily, the entire afternoon would pass by without us seeing them again until near suppertime. Myrna and I ate when we chose, swam until our skin was water-wrinkled, and lay beneath the hot rays of the sun without lotion unless we felt inclined to put it on. We'd swim deep into the black waters onto the wooden raft far from shore, near the buoys bobbing in the lake, then to the break wall and past the moorings of the pier where the *Canadiana* docked.

About four in the afternoon the steamship would make a wide, final arc and head straight toward Crystal Beach. Seeing her on the horizon, wordlessly my sister and I would shake out our blanket, gather our things and start for home. We didn't do this because we were instructed to, but because we wanted to take our showers before Majestic guests returned from the beach.

The cottage had old-fashioned water tanks. Myrna would gently turn on the gas, then ignite the pilot light with a wooden match to heat the water. If you weren't among the first to bathe, you risked showering in tepid water.

Dad lived in Buffalo during the work week but returned to Crystal Beach every Friday night on the *Canadiana*. We didn't see him for five long days. Myrna and I would dash through the park to make sure we were there when the boat docked on Friday night. I felt the United States was a world away, yet it only took Dad one hour and fifteen minutes to sail from the dusty streets of Buffalo to the sands of Crystal Beach.

Sunday was our favorite day of the week. "Shh," Dad said one morning as he shook me awake. Just as stealthily he woke Myrna. "Hurry and get dressed," he whispered, and we needed no prodding. In the rustic bathroom of the cottage, we pushed and poked one another as we washed our sleepy faces and swished toothbrushes about. After a quick glimpse into the mirror, my sister and I were ready to embark on a Sunday with Dad.

It was close to six-thirty in the morning when we slipped away. Of paramount importance was that we be extremely quiet so as not to disturb our sleeping guests at the Majestic. Dad laid a shushing finger to his lips as we carefully made our way past the squeaky porch door and tiptoed down the concrete steps. When we got to the road, Dad grabbed our hands and swung them jubilantly in the air. How sweet our freedom.

Down the deserted streets we walked through the park in the direction of the concrete pier where the *Canadiana* docked. Ordinarily a scene of bedlam, this early in the morning everything was quiet and serene. The wharf itself was barely visible, blurred and veiled beneath a silver film of grey. The only persons about were a few stone-faced fishermen casting off into the lake.

Vaguely aware of waves slapping the break wall and the spray of water on our faces, we peered out at the sky, anxious for the early morning fog to dissipate. On the horizon appeared a minute bead of fire. The speck grew larger and larger. Slowly hues of orchid, pink, orange and blue eradicated the last vestiges of the night. As the sun rose, we witnessed the birthing of a new day. Our trio sat in rapt silence squinting in the brilliance of the sun's emergence.

We followed a steep path down to the shoreline intending to walk to Bayside Beach, less than two miles away, yet it always took at least an hour for us to get there. This was not a hike but rather a leisurely, meandering stroll in the early morning.

Once there, we cast off our sandals and dipped our toes in the cool waves as they hit the beach. We shared some stale bread brought from home, shredded into small pieces so we could feed the flock of sea gulls that clustered about us. For a few minutes Myrna and I were surrounded by a circle of fluttering white feathers and frenzied, maniacal shrieking birds, and when the food was gone, so were they.

A four-foot stone fence lined the rear of the beach and we sat there silently watching the ebb and flow of the waves. By tacit agreement, early morning beach goers just nodded their heads to one another in cursory recognition. Nothing other than the sounds of nature had any part to play in the sublime tranquility we were feeling.

Workman on the beach raked sand into neat, ridged rows and emptied trash cans. Vendors dragged webbed chairs and umbrellas closer to shore. A Snack Hut employee rolled up the eatery's shutters, pulled down a striped, blue canopy, then hosed the sand away from the front of the food stand. On the horizon, small boats bobbed up and down. The beach was waking up.

Each Sunday morning, we ate breakfast in front of Schmidt's bakery, seated on white steel-mesh chairs around a white table. Although we loved the sugar donuts oozing raspberry filling, it was always a challenge to eat them neatly. Despite small nibbles, despite the use of many napkins, despite our best intentions, raspberry juice dribbled down our chins.

Suddenly, I glanced over at Dad. It was now nearing ten o'clock in the morning. Dad's light brown hair was disheveled from the lake's breeze. His blue eyes were partially closed as he shielded them against the glare of sunlight. He was smoking his first cigarette of the day and sipping coffee. When I caught his eye, he smiled at Myrna and me so intensely, so lovingly, I felt my eyes well up. Could I have somehow known then that this was one of those special moments I would always remember?

Too soon, the sidewalk began to fill with the hustle and bustle of people on a mission. Many were looking for a place to eat. Others were in a hurry to get to the park. Some were determined to go to the beach. People were pushing strollers, walking pets; everyone was burdened with packages, everyone seemed rushed, harried.

Somewhere a baby cried, a dog barked, and church bells sounded nearby. Automobiles with Canadian and American plates crowded the street. A Greyhound bus brought traffic to a near standstill. Inevitably, an impatient driver pressed hard on his horn, and then soon another driver did the same. We glanced at each other with sadness. The time to leave had come; we headed for home.

Many of our cottage guests were not even dressed yet, just lingering over coffee, scanning the newspaper, enjoying a leisurely Sunday morning. We burst through the doors smelling of the lake, dusted with sand, our skin tinged pink from the sun, and someone would invariably ask, "Where do you all go so early in the morning?"

Myrna and I would grin at each other and simultaneously answer, "Oh, no place special."

I always winked at Dad then, so he'd know we were just kidding.

Once our cottage became more popular, more in demand, our parents became much busier. I seldom got a bedroom to myself anymore and those wonderful Sunday morning jaunts with our father became rarer and rarer.

4
A Tough Cookie

My mother's new role as proprietor of the Majestic cottage at Crystal Beach required her to step up to the challenges of operating a boarding house. She found many of her tenants recalcitrant adults who thought her cottage was a home away from home without any of the responsibilities. There was no way she was going to put up with this nonsense. Rules were needed.

Dad came up with the brilliant idea of file card messages. The first one appeared in the kitchens. "PLEASE CLEAN UP AFTER YOURSELF." Unfortunately, this was misconstrued as a request to do so only if you felt so inclined. Coffee grounds clung to the percolator. Dishes were washed, yet remained on the dryer rack, garbage wasn't taken out. Her next sign made its debut on a larger piece of cardboard and was far more specific. "LEAVE THE KITCHEN NEAT." There was no *please* in that sentence.

Soon more reminders appeared in strategic areas. In the bathrooms: "PUT TOILET SEAT DOWN" and in the bedrooms: "NO EATING ALLOWED." "USE REAR DOOR ONLY" guided tenants returning from the beach. Should someone forget her directions, Mother would kindly remind them, always with a slight smile on her face, yet with eyes as hard as marbles.

As the years went by, the Majestic's reputation grew as a superior place to stay and with good reason. For a beach cottage it was remarkably clean. Weekdays, Mother rose early to mop the communal areas with a bleach and water solution. She scoured the bathrooms, dusted furniture and watered her plants before anyone else was awake in the cottage.

With limited space in both refrigerators and shared cupboards, we brought food in as needed. Thus, there were always a few trips to local vendors included in our morning errands. No direct mail delivery to the individual cottages existed, so a daily trip to the post office was crucial. Most requests for reservations at the Majestic came to us this way.

Although treated cordially, our tenants were not Mother's friends. She was their landlady. They respectfully referred to her as Missus or Mrs. Zarne. Of course, all the people at the cottage liked our dad much better. The husbands went fishing with him, discussed sports, and played poker with Dad every Friday night. He was a most congenial fellow, so unlike his wife.

Mother was strict, aloof and bossy, and there were times she had no choice but to be so, such as the last week of July and the first week of August. We were at maximum occupancy allowed by our innkeepers' license. People were everywhere and our resources were strained to the limit.

One late afternoon during this frenetic time, Mother returned from the beach to the cottage with young Linda and was confronted with the aromatic smell of spaghetti sauce bubbling in a large pot on the stove. Mrs. Silver, one of our tenants, had been at it for quite some time as the kitchen was already steamy and hot. Her daughter was preoccupied with transforming a large mound of hamburger into a great many small meat balls. The amount of food being prepared was far more than could be consumed by the two people Mother had rented one room to.

There was no sign banning lengthy food preparation or the entertainment of personal guests. It was simply unthinkable that anyone would presume they could do this at any time but especially so when the Majestic was in the throes of its two busiest weeks of the summer. As my mother stared silent and aghast, Mrs. Silver said nervously, "Oh Hi Missus. I invited my daughter's family over for dinner tonight and we're goin' to eat spaghetti out on the patio."

She smiled disarmingly. "I promise to leave everything spic and span." Mrs. Silver had already monopolized the kitchen and now intended to intrude on our scant backyard space.

Mother shook her head from side to side. "No! No!" she shouted adamantly, flailing her arms about. "You absolutely cannot do this. Where did you ever get the idea that you could? Clean this all up and get your sauce off the stove now."

"C'mon, Mrs. Zarne, I made the sauce from scratch and it has to be heated up somewhere. I have five extra people comin' over, for dinner," Mrs. Silver pleaded. "Where else can we possibly go?"

Tenants, recently returned from the beach, congregated in the back yard curious to hear what the ruckus was. Obviously, there was some kind of disagreement going on. Voices were not raised to this level at the Majestic.

Mother was livid. "Go to the park! Take them out for dinner! Throw it in the garbage." Her voice rose with each sentence. "I absolutely do not care. You rented one room with me not an entire cottage. You've been cooking all day. It's sweltering in here. How on earth could you ever think this would be okay?" she asked incredulously.

Mrs. Silver stood there staring at my mother, slack jawed. Clearly, she thought there would be some understanding of her predicament and hadn't expected this explosive a reaction. "I want you to know," she volleyed back, now indignant. "You've put me in a terrible fix, Mrs. Zarne. I'm going to leave tomorrow and will expect a full refund," she said haughtily.

As Mother exited the kitchen, she laughed. "Leave! Please leave! You signed a 'No Refund' clause when we rented to you."

Suddenly the front door swung open. There stood Mrs. Silver's brawny son-in-law and three young boys home from the beach, dragging wet towels across the parlor floor, sand in their hair, lake water dripping from their bodies. "It looks like we got here just in time to get our showers before the hordes descend," he joked with a big toothy smile. The hordes he referred to were our regulars already waiting out in the backyard.

34

Although Mother was dwarfed by this large man, she would not be deterred. Coldly she announced, "Your mother-in-law has overstepped. She had no business inviting you all here to the cottage. You'll have to find somewhere else to wash up and eat your supper."

"Hey, Missus," the son-in-law growled, "No need to be nasty. Just let me and the kids take quick showers and we'll be out of here as soon as we're done eating."

"No," Mother said. "You can't use my showers and you can't eat in my backyard." She pointed her finger at him. "You have no rights here. I want you all out immediately."

"Hey Missus," he said, eyes narrowed as he advanced toward her. "I'd say that's a bit harsh. I'd say maybe you should reconsider."

"And I'm saying," she snapped back, eyes blazing, "you're trespassing on private property and I'm calling the police." My God, the woman was fearless, I thought.

She grabbed Linda, herded Myrna and me into her bedroom, and bolted the door with a flimsy hook and eye lock. Now, temper spent, she sat on the bed, body shaking, nervously wringing her hands, questioning if her fury had thrust us all in danger. The son-in-law was a big, surly man and she was here all alone.

We could hear their angry, outraged voices cursing our mother from outside the door, the sound of clanging pots, slamming cupboards, heavy stomping on the stairs. After thirty minutes or so, it sounded as if they had finally decided to pack it in as the screen door was opened and slammed closed several times. With relief, we finally heard car motors screeching away. Suddenly all was quiet, yet we all lingered in the bedroom a while longer to make sure they weren't going to change their minds and come back.

Mother rinsed her face, combed her hair, and changed into fresh clothes. Somewhat calmer, she left our sanctuary and strode into the main area of the cottage, smiling, head held high. Her authoritarian demeanor, while shaky, was still intact. If anyone in the past had any doubts Mrs. Zarne ran a tight ship, those thoughts were now surely obliterated. As she entered the kitchen to begin preparing dinner, it was with great satisfaction she saw that Mrs. Silver had cleaned up her mess and all was orderly.

Mother's ominous threat of contacting the police must have alarmed them enough to make their exit, yet of course, it had all been a bluff. There was no way our mother could have possibly accomplished that task since there was no telephone service hooked up to the Majestic until five years later. Fortunately, on that particular day, no one was aware of it.

5
Stormy Weather

The worst thing that could happen to the folks staying at the Majestic was to suffer a stormy day, yet when rain came, it was always my mother who suffered most grievously. She would have awakened early to the sound of strong, pulsating sheets of rain smashing against the rooftop. At first, she might have thought it was just a cloudburst, but raising the shade above her window, any hope of that was immediately dashed.

Outside, a tempest raged, causing lightning strikes to crisscross the sky and torrential rain to course down relentlessly. I imagined it was with herculean effort that she got herself out of bed and dressed for the day. Rainstorms were extremely disturbing to her because even though it was irrational, she knew our guests would hold her personally responsible for the awful weather.

As soon as Mother opened the door to her bedroom, she could see people were already in a bad mood. Everyone was still clad in their night clothes, wandering about in a daze, angrily staring out the windows with dismay. Surely a curse had come upon them for this to happen while they were on holiday.

Mother was assailed by one of the sullen women.

"Missus," she said accusingly, "it's raining again. You know this is the second time since I've been here?"

Mother hadn't even had her first cup of coffee yet. "Sorry," she growled, "I don't make the weather." With a clarity borne of experience she knew that obvious statement, "It's raining again," was going to be delivered to her time and time again before this dreadful day ended.

Crystal Beach was rendered helpless, isolated, literally cut off at the knees by storms such as this one. The *S.S. Canadiana* cancelled her crossings from Buffalo and the park completely closed down. Here at the Majestic, our guests' options were extremely limited when we were all clustered together. The few communal areas of the cottage were small.

Husbands who only came out to the beach for weekends needed their cars for work, thus leaving their wives and children powerless to flee this nightmare scenario. The cottage guests became morose and crankier as the morning hours passed and no change appeared in the weather. Previous plans were cancelled. Our surly visitors had lost a precious day of their vacation. They were held hostage by the elements of nature.

And as always, the most convenient scapegoat was Missus Zarne, all powerful, all knowing owner of the Majestic. This kind of day was my mother's Achilles heel, the chink in her armor, her moment in time as the impotent Wizard of Oz behind the green curtain. They had expected Missus Zarne to provide pleasant weather along with fresh sheets, and she had failed.

Everyone kept peering out the windows, hoping for a different result, but all signs pointed to the storm lingering or about to grow worse. This deluge was not going to end anytime soon. Already the road on our street was flooded and branches had fallen from trees. Because of the severe lightning strikes, it was extremely dangerous to go outside. All who dwelt at the Majestic became captive within its walls. "Stay inside and stay safe," Mrs. Zarne chanted often and sadly.

After lunch, I watched her reluctantly take on the role of recreational director. Most of her tenants were women, so she permitted them to play card games or Mahjong in the parlor even though doing this monopolized the only room in the cottage that was not utilitarian. Many mothers encouraged their children to entertain themselves with board games out on the porch. This soon proved impossible as the torrential rain blew in from all directions, rendering the veranda completely uninhabitable.

When the parents, in desperation, finally relegated their offspring to their bedrooms, Missus Zarne brought out her special, last ditch, rainy day, secret weapon. It was a large cardboard box filled with dogeared, mostly coverless, comic books. She had collected the most popular ones of those years: *Superman, Archie, Mad, Wonder Woman, Amazing Spider-man, Captain America, Tales from the Crypt, Thor, Iron Man, The Hulk,* and other popular Marvel heroes. The kids were enthralled and captivated, reading and rereading the same stories for hours. Many parents did not allow their children to read comic books in their own homes, but no one objected that day at all. Those who sincerely sought solitude were truly most afflicted, griping the loudest and rightfully so, as they truly had nowhere to go to escape the bedlam.

Windows and doors, shut tightly, kept out the downpour, but too soon the air in the cottage became stagnant and steamy. The humidity reached so high a level that the air felt heavy and sodden and everything one touched felt sticky.

I always thought Mother felt guilty about this dreadful situation, especially as she and Dad had never made provisions for these catastrophic times. While unrealistic, their hope that everyone would be mostly outdoors during the daytime hours enjoying themselves was foolish. No space was designated for situations like this. A few years back, my parents had chosen to build two extra bedrooms plus a half bath at the rear of the cottage. They felt it was far more practical than having a recreational room that would be used only rarely. I wondered if they regretted that decision.

By midafternoon, Mother's solution to her rainy day wretchedness was to hibernate in the furthest away bedroom of our two-room suite. She'd listen to the radio or better still take a nap after inserting ear plugs into her ears and locking her door securely. Outside our rooms was an ominous sign reading "DO NOT DISTURB."

Even the most privileged, her children, dared not tap on that door unless the cottage was on fire or the world had been knocked off its orbit. When Mrs. Zarne's private areas were completely shut tight like this, and that black block-printed sign was pinned up, it meant she was at the end of her rope and would tolerate nothing more. The ominous warning might as well have proclaimed, "Abandon all hope ye who enter here."

About five o'clock, Mother finally emerged from her refuge looking drained. She was bent over from the stress of the day's events. Stormy weather always brought her low; she said it was the millstone round her neck, the thorn in her side, her own personal flavor of Kryptonite.

Hour after hour, rain pelted the cottage mercilessly. Someone jokingly questioned whether we should all get busy and begin building an ark, yet no one laughed or even chuckled. Late afternoon, when it seemed things couldn't possibly get any worse, the lights began to flicker and fears rose about losing electricity. Each time the lights quivered even slightly, anxiety levels ratcheted up significantly. There was extreme concern about people groping about in the dark, hot food spills, or someone taking an unfortunate fall, especially where there were steps no one was able see. The cottage had already darkened prematurely from the steel gray skies outside.

Out came Mother's cache of flashlights and lanterns. She distributed a few to each family and set up extras in strategic spots. Cooking privileges were suspended. Mother locked the shower room doors. She was in emergency mode and no one dared complain when her edicts were activated. Instinctively, they all felt Mrs. Zarne would know what to do. They trusted her to make wise decisions that would keep them safe. Throughout that bleak, sopping, miserable day and night, the one positive thought everyone could hold fast to was that Mrs. Zarne was at the helm.

Our sorry tenants slept restlessly that night, unconvinced that they had the ability to endure one more muggy, dreary day trapped inside the Majestic. Mother later admitted she had cravenly considered catching a bus to Buffalo with the three of us if the monsoon did not come to a halt. Only after indulging gleeful thoughts of abandoning all of her tenants, Mother admitted, was she finally calm enough to fall asleep.

As we slumbered, flooded roads dried, winds died down, and the storm fled as swiftly as it had come. The temperature inched upwards to the seventies by mid-morning. Mother opened wide the windows. A welcomed breeze from the lake fluttered through and ruffled the kitchen curtains. The sun grazed her cheeks. By noon everyone was out of the cottage.

As she sipped her second cup of coffee, Mother looked very satisfied with herself and the decision made all those years ago. The Majestic now had two extra bedrooms and another half bath instead of a recreation room that would be only used occasionally.

She had no need to second guess herself for such a brilliant move. Somehow, as always, everyone had gotten through the wretched day unscathed.

6
Wicked Doings

Mother would don a dress, hat, high heels and board the streetcar to downtown Buffalo, New York, for shopping and lunch every Saturday morning when we weren't living out at the Majestic. She would alternate taking her daughters with her for company and would stop to eat at different luncheonettes. These were eateries with lengthy narrow counters and brightly colored swivel stools. The waitresses wore pastel-colored uniforms, white frilly aprons, and cute pointed hat pieces that matched. They carried minty green pads to write down customers' orders and would ask, "Whatjawant?"

The items available were limited to mostly sandwiches, drinks, and a choice of pies. We waved the menu away because we always knew exactly what we wanted, which was, of course, the bacon, lettuce and tomato club sandwiches. The BLTs came with toothpicks impaled into each quadrant to keep all the ingredients from bursting out and a side helping of potato chips, and we loved them. Even though eating pork was something our Jewish faith renounced, we mentally removed bacon from that taboo list. Conversly, upon taking occupancy of the Majestic, Dad had hung a religious amulet called a *mezuzah* to the front door. Handwritten on a parchment scroll was a blessing inserted inside the black *mezuzah* for peace and protection to all who dwelt in the the house.

Dad was good-natured about our Friday night movies and Saturday shopping excursions, as he was easy-going about most things. However, he was adamant that no bacon be served inside our house although he was aware we ate it when we were in restaurants. Mother nodded, "I totally agree with you one hundred percent," she said, "except, of course when we're at the Majestic in Crystal Beach, Canada is on foreign soil and of course, different rules apply." She was ever the negotiator.

A strange pattern emerged when we came out in spring to clean and ready the Majestic for the summer. Mother would rummage through her pocketbook for a couple colorful Canadian dollars. She'd give these to Myrna so she could make haste to the grocery store for some urgently needed supplies. Every weekend it was the same: milk, bread, some veggies, chips and bacon. Smack in the kitchen of the Majestic, our mother intended to make us BLTs for lunch. Dad's ears would perk up at the mention of the word *bacon*, but he said nothing because, as Mother had explained, we were on foreign soil.

In order to avoid any unnecessary discussion with Dad about it, when Myrna returned with our groceries, Mother announced very clearly and loudly, "I'm taking the bacon to the laundry room," as if it were a naughty child. There she had a double burner hot plate stored in our minuscule, windowless laundry room, along with a couple frying pans and a spatula. It was tacitly understood that's where the bacon was going to be prepared. The pungent aroma remained trapped inside the laundry room and lingered in the surrounding air long after it had been cooked, a mute reminder of what she had done.

My sisters and I were busy in the kitchen prepping vegetables, while Dad made hot cocoa from scratch. Once the sizzling bacon was brought in, we assembled our sandwiches on white bread freshly toasted and slathered them with mayo. Dad nibbled on his humdrum tuna salad while the rest of us reveled in our forbidden feast. These wicked doings continued throughout the spring without a glitch.

During the second weekend in June while we were indulging in our sumptuous lunch, Dad spied a blue Chevrolet parking directly in front of our cottage. No alarms went off as we never had visitors this early in the season. That is, until Dad recognized them.

"Oh, my God," he exclaimed. "It's Harold and Evie!" The Kramers were our next-door neighbors in Buffalo. Because it was a beautiful spring day, they had decided to pay us an impromptu visit. The Kramers were far more religious than us. Although we never claimed to be as observant as they were, it would have been embarrassing if they caught us eating those verboten sandwiches.

Mother shouted, "Harry, keep them outside as long as you can while we clean up in here. Open the windows! Open the windows!" she commanded, flailing her arms about for emphasis, even though the windows were already opened. She gathered an armful of sandwiches into her apron, and stuffed them into the kitchen oven, but in her frenzy, dropped a sandwich. It smashed open and all the fixings inside spilt out and fell to the linoleum. I grabbed a dish rag and dropped down to the floor to clean up the spill even as it expanded into an ever-widening greasy circle.

In her harried effort to clear away all traces of our lunch from the kitchen table, Myrna accidentally spilt an entire mug of cocoa. The sweet syrupy drink, fortunately warm, not hot, wasn't only dripping down onto the linoleum but into my hair and onto my shoulders as I toiled feverishly on the slithery mess below. Dad gallantly kept the Kramers at bay, first on the sidewalk with small talk, then to the backyard to show off our newest improvements, and after that back to the shade of the porch. We were in crisis mode in the kitchen, mere footsteps away from where they kibitzed on the veranda.

After doing everything we possibly could to erase all traces of our transgressions, Mother said she felt brave enough to receive them. "Quick take off your apron," I whispered as it still reeked of her covert activities.

"Linda," I instructed our youngest sister, "quick. Get rid of this," pointing to the offensive object. Thankfully, she removed the smelly apron from the kitchen, and I rushed over to the sink frantic to rinse the sticky cocoa out of my hair.

Mother invited the Kramers into the parlor, albeit reluctantly. "Harry!" she admonished my father, "Bring Evelyn and Harold in already. I'll make some tea." She was ever the gracious hostess. Outwardly, she appeared poised, relaxed, seemingly unruffled by their surprise social call but we, her family, knew this was a guise. Mother was all shook up.

As they sat there sipping their drinks, Mrs. Kramer's nose began twitching. "I smell bacon," Evelyn Kramer said adamantly. "If I didn't know any better," her voice rose, "I would say it's coming right from here." She continued to sniff the air with diligence.

"Oh, silly Evie," Mother said with a poker face, "you fancy you have a nose like a bloodhound. You're mistaken. I can't smell anything like that at all."

Evelyn sat up straight in her chair, thrust her chin forward, her nostrils quivered. "My nose knows what my nose knows." She announced as her pointer finger stabbed the air for emphasis.

"Maybe it's coming from outside," Mother conceded wearily, suddenly aware that Linda had draped the foul apron neatly over a chair close to where Mr. Kramer sat. The visit was strained, yet they stayed an exceptionally long time, drinking cup after cup of tea and nibbling English biscuits.

Mrs. Kramer probably didn't believe Mother's explanation regarding the permeating odor of bacon in the cottage, but nothing was amiss in that spotless kitchen to indicate anything objectionable had been cooked there. The odor had finally begun to dissipate a bit, or possibly we had all just gotten used to it. They finally left and even before the Kramer's car turned the corner away from the cottage, we retrieved our cold sandwiches from the oven and set them back on the table. Although not nearly as tasty as they had once been, we still devoured them.

"Good grief", Mother said. "What nerve to come over just like that without being asked."

"I thought they'd never leave," Dad added.

"That Evie is such a snoop," Mother said.

"That was one close call," Dad said as he cleared away the dishes.

Mother agreed wholeheartedly. "I would have been so embarrassed if she had caught us eating those BLTs. Thank goodness I cooked it up in the laundry room."

"Luckily there was no way for Evie to pinpoint for sure where the smell was coming from," Dad assured her. "She sure did her best, though, short of opening the oven." He chuckled.

"Evie is the most hypocritical person I know, and without a doubt, the world's biggest blabbermouth," Mother added self-righteously.

Dad suggested softly, "Maybe the time has come to stop bringing bacon into the Majestic even if it happens to be in Canada."

Mother nodded her head thoughtfully. "Maybe," she conceded most amiably.

They sighed in unison.

"But on the other hand," she chirped, "I just don't have the heart to disappoint the kids. You know how much they look forward to their BLTs."

7
A Handful Of Handers

From the moment the Handers arrived for their two-week stay, Mother knew she had made a dire mistake by allowing them into the Majestic.

The family had rented two bedrooms at the top of the staircase for themselves and their children, a boy of seven and a girl of nine. Their kids were wild and completely uncontrollable. They'd run through the cottage, bump into furniture and crash into people. Mother would stop them when she saw them misbehaving, but she wasn't always around.

One time they ran smack into Mrs. Blatnik and toppled her to the floor while she was carrying soup to the kitchen table. Fortunately, the soup that spilt wasn't that hot, but the lady had bruises the next day and was very angry at the Handers, especially their mother, who made light of the incident.

Their stuff was left all over the cottage. The girl liked to dress in the major bathroom yet always left her pajamas, robe and towels carelessly tossed all over the bathroom. Other tenants were constantly tripping over the boy's shoes or sneakers or toys. Everywhere Mother looked were things that belonged to the Handers: socks, caps, eyeglasses, and beach bags. Their possessions were draped over chairs, on the porch, in the kitchen. The Handers abandoned their mess wherever they happened to be when they were finished with them.

After many ignored reminders, Mother resigned herself to gathering everything that was theirs into a basket she left near the laundry room. Nightly she'd remind them to retrieve their basket before they went upstairs to their rooms at the end of the day.

Sunday would mark the end of their first week with us, and everyone in the cottage was counting down the days when the Handers would be leaving. Mother kept reassuring herself that she could put up with anything for only seven more days. Their odds and ends basket was filling up fast just with items she had collected that morning. With what she had collected so far, it was overflowing when she moved it from the entranceway of our small laundry room. Sighing, Mother moved it out of the way to a corner in the backyard, to a place where it wouldn't interfere with our work that day.

Sunday was our laundry and moving-in day, and it exhausted us all. Dad would toil along with Mother, collecting sheets from vacated bedrooms so they could be laundered before our three o'clock check-in guests arrived.

The Majestic had one washer that chugged across the laundry room floor, struggling to accommodate the large loads Mother fed it. Dad hung the damp sheets on rope lines in the backyard, sticking slender wood poles under the lines to lift them high. They swung in the wind, bleaching in the sun and when my parents put them on the beds, the sheets ushered in the scent of the outdoors.

When the clothes were slightly damp, Myrna and I ironed them on a piece of equipment called a mangle. The machine was electrically connected to the laundry room and placed on a table in the backyard. We'd sit before the machine guiding double layers of fabric through the hissing mangle's pads by sections. Although it was tedious work, in minutes the sheets emerged wrinkle free and crisp.

It was a point of pride to our mother to make up the beds with air dried sheets as a special welcome to our new guests. As the last of the laundry finished drying, we were all able to finally take a much needed break.

Once all the sheets were dried, we'd take the clotheslines down and return that and any other equipment we had used that day to their home in the laundry room. We needed to tidy up quickly so the backyard would be ready for tenants who wanted to eat their suppers outside. Sunday was the most arduous, grueling day of the week for my family. This was the price we paid to enjoy the other six.

That particular Sunday afternoon, when the Handers returned from the beach, their kids remained in the backyard as their mother prepared lunch. Those ingenious children had just invented a new game. They ran about the backyard, in and out between the sheets, lurking behind them, pulling the sheets down on themselves and using them as capes as they played a rampant game of hide and seek. Mother heard the ruckus, the shouting and shrill laughter, so she went out back to see what was happening and such a sight it was.

The slender wood poles that held the laundry high had been knocked down by the Hander kids' rough play. They used the white sheets to hide behind and then run through. The sheets had been wrenched from the clotheslines and lay in heaps on the ground, grass stained and dirty as though they had been stomped on.

"You two sit right there." Mother was outraged. "I want your parents to see exactly what you've been doing out here," and she summoned them outside to see why she was so angry. Her voice cracking, Mother said, "Look at what damage your children have done. We've been doing laundry since early today and these were the very last things that needed drying."

"I'm very sorry," Mrs. Handers said to her, most sincerely, "but kids are kids. I know they meant no harm."

Mother was furious. "I thought we were finally done and now it's all got to be done again. I'd appreciate it if you took care of getting these sheets washed at the laundromat. What happened is your responsibility."

"What are you talking about?" Mrs. Hander asked astonished. "This was an accident, and you can't blame me."

"Your kids had no business running through here," Dad admonished. "They were out of control."

"Those were clean sheets and now they're filthy," Mother added, stunned at their lack of remorse.

"Nonsense," Mr. Hander said nonchalantly. "They're not all that soiled. They're still usable."

"The sheets are filthy," Mother said. "And need to be washed again. You should take care of doing it."

"Hey, I'm sorry about this, but we certainly don't intend to do anything of the sort," Mr. Hander said, "Your cottage. Your problem. We're on vacation." And they and their children walked brazenly out of the yard.

Mother said nothing more, but she was fuming. Myrna and I went off to spend what was left of our afternoon at the laundromat. Dad began checking in our new arrivals and Mother prepared the last of the bedrooms with sets of spare sheets bereft of outdoor freshness.

All through dinner Mother was very quiet, brooding over what had happened. Many of our tenants sympathized with her and talked about the atrocious behavior of the Handers' kids in hushed tones. It was shocking to them that the parents had dismissed the incident so callously when their children were so clearly responsible.

It was ten-thirty in the evening when the Handers returned for the night. My parents barely acknowledged them. The atmosphere was frosty, and the Handers made a hasty retreat up to their bedrooms. No one remembered their basket of belongings left outside.

At eleven o'clock, as usual, Dad locked all the doors and left a porch light on to usher home any latecomers. Most everyone was settled in for the night.

Our family quarters had two adjoining bedrooms and about midnight, I heard Mother slip out of her room. As I hadn't fallen asleep yet, I got out of bed to join her.

"Maybe some hot milk will help you fall asleep," I said as I filled a small pot of milk to heat for the two of us, and once it was warm enough, we made our way to the outside patio.

"I just can't get over their behavior today. It won't stop replaying in my head," Mother sighed as she sat down on one of the chairs.

I, too, was angry at the cavalier way Mother had been treated. Most everyone at the Majestic was respectful of her and Dad. What the Handers had done was outrageous. Once we were settled, gentle raindrops began to fall on the canvas awning. The rhythmic sounds of the rain and the smell of fresh grass were actually quite soothing. I felt my mother calming down a bit as we sat there.

Suddenly she shouted, "Their stuff is going to get drenched." She had remembered that she had taken the Handers' basket of belongings from the laundry room and moved it aside to the yard. She jumped up from her chair, intending to rescue the basket; surely it was getting wetter and wetter by the minute.

Abruptly she stopped. Mother sat herself back down under the shelter of the canopy. She leisurely sipped her milk and listened to the rain continue to fall, now much heavier. She closed her eyes, a grin on her face. When we returned to our bedrooms, I felt confident Mother would now sleep well.

When the Handers recovered their sodden basket the next day, all their things in it were drenched. Even though old newspapers were the first things tossed away, some of the print had bled through onto their clothes. The dirty sneakers their kids had left strewn about caused further grime, and it was questionable if the book Mrs. Handley had been reading could be salvaged. The pages were stuck together as if they had been glued shut.

Mr. and Mrs. Hander were furious with Mother for leaving their basket out in the rain instead of carefully returning it to the laundry room, as any prudent landlord would do. Because of her irresponsibility, they shouted, their plans were ruined, and they now were doomed to spending the better part of a perfectly beautiful summer afternoon replacing their ruined items and laundering wet clothes.

Mother listened to their litany of complaints stoically. When she had endured enough of their tirade, she turned her back on them and began to leave the backyard. "Where do you think you're going?" Mr. Hander shrieked. "This is unacceptable. What are you going to do about it?"

Mother turned so she faced them directly. Her eyes narrowed and enunciating each word carefully so there could be no mistaking what she was saying, she informed them in her sweet voice, "Your basket. Your problem."

8
Wolf Comes To Dinner

My sister and I were quite excited because our grandparents, Wolf and Yetta, were coming over for dinner on Friday night to our cottage in Canada. We hadn't gotten together for a long time, probably last at Thanksgiving, and now it was nearly the end of June.

There had been a hushed conversation between my parents earlier that day. I spied my mother in a corner of the kitchen sniffling, my dad's arm draped about her. Intuitively, I knew not to interrupt this scene, but it baffled me.

My mother's soup still bubbled on the stove. She had cooked a brisket along with vegetables and prepared the salad, now chilling in the refrigerator. She had covered the table with a white cloth. A fresh bread that my sister and I bought earlier that day lay beneath a matching napkin. Dad had poured red wine into a glass decanter to be served during dinner.

As soon as Grandma and Grandpa walked into the cottage, my sister and I rushed to welcome them. Why so much time had elapsed since we had seen them was a mystery, but at last they were here now to eat supper with us. We called Yetta Grandma, even though she was really our step-grandma. Yetta had married Wolf years ago and had brought up his four children after Dad's mother died. We loved her all the same. And she was ecstatic to be with us. She clasped my mother, my sisters and me close to her, hugging and kissing us, while effusively thanking Mother for inviting them over.

Wolf, as always, was remote. No cuddly Grandpa was our grandpa. The first thing one noticed about him were his piercing blue eyes, a trait my father had inherited. Wolf was neither tall nor short, neither fat nor thin. With pure white hair, he was a very nice-looking man with an aura of kindness about him, like a judge or a man of God. It was this compassionate shell he reserved for the world yet denied his family. Grandpa strode into the living room, his stance rigid and tense. No kisses, hugs or words for any of us. His eyes darted from side to side. He seemed twitchy and nervous.

"Come! Come! Sit!" smiled my father, leading them to the sofa. As Dad poured iced tea for everyone, his hands trembled a bit. We sipped our drinks in silence. Grandma Yetta, good humored as ever, laughed and attempted to make small talk. Wolf sat far back in his chair, arms crossed, uncommunicative, a grimace on his face.

During dinner the atmosphere was stilted and unnatural. We ate with limited conversation, so unlike our boisterous family meals. As we neared the end of the meal, Mother leaned back in her chair, visibly relaxing, as she slowly sipped red wine.

Grandfather Wolf uttered the only words he had spoken to anyone since his arrival. "How are you feeling now?" He was addressing me.

At first, I thought it an odd question but then remembered I hadn't seen him since early December when I was rushed to the hospital by ambulance.

"Yeah! I'm doing okay," I whispered. His question forced me to recall the unhappy time when my appendix ruptured and peritonitis set in. Dad's mother, Wolf's first wife, had died when she was in her thirties from the same condition. My poor father had entered my hospital room, pasty white and terrified I would suffer the same fate as his mother. Unaware of how sick I was, how grave my situation, I constantly pleaded to go home. My mother, who was not religious, prayed all the time for me. I was nine years old. The doctor had already informed my parents to be prepared for an unfavorable outcome.

I remember being in a hospital bed surrounded with steel rails, intubated, and constantly poked and prodded. The loneliness and discomfort of those scary days were intensified by the cheery preparations for the forthcoming Christmas holiday. My room was decorated by nice nurses who had put up a tree. Jolly carolers stopped by. Santa visited and left toys and dolls for me, yet I was too sick to feel any joy.

Slowly, incredibly, I began to recover, even though it had been very questionable whether I would. Discharged after six weeks in the hospital, the slow recuperation at home continued for two months more, before I was strong enough to return to my third-grade class in March.

I heard Grandpa say, "You're a very lucky girl to be alive." His words brought me acutely back to the present, "Especially with the kind of mother you have!"

The room went silent as the shock of what Wolf had just said sunk in. Mother sat motionless, holding the almost full glass of wine she had been sipping, mid-air. Yetta gasped. Dad stared at his father horrorstruck. I wondered if somehow, I had misunderstood Grandpa's words.

"Why did you even come?" Mother whispered as she rose from the table and flung the wine she had been drinking into Wolf's face. Blood-like rivulets streamed down his beard staining the white shirt he was wearing. Dad yanked his father from the chair he had been sitting on, and the chair crashed to the floor. "Out you go," Dad ordered as he dragged his father toward the front door.

"Wolf! Wolf! What's wrong with you?" Grandma Yetta shrieked. "You're lucky they even let you in their house after everything you've done and said. Have you completely lost your mind?" she wailed.

Grandpa lifted himself up from the floor, and then walked away from the carnage, a snicker on his face. Dad was flushed and his fists were clenched. We could hear our mother crying in the bedroom. What on earth had just happened?

Dad downplayed the evening's events the next day, explaining that Wolf and Mother had just never gotten along. Myrna and I nodded our heads, but we really didn't believe this story he had woven, and the forthcoming events confirmed our doubts. Wolf was never again invited to the Majestic or into our home in Buffalo. No longer was he included in holiday celebrations or milestone events. The bitterness between Wolf and our mother was now etched in acid and could never be erased.

Grandma Yetta was bereft over Wolf's conduct. We adored our effervescent Grandma, yet now saw her a great deal less than in the past. It was an enormous loss, but Wolf had become a pariah.

Despite Dad's initial fury, he continued to try to be a good son. A couple times a year, he would gather my sisters and me together to visit his father, so the man would know his grandchildren. Grandpa would sit solemnly at his kitchen table, ignoring us completely. When those dreadful visits ended, we'd kiss him dutifully and his beard would scratch our faces.

My sisters and I had no idea what had motivated Grandpa Wolf to blurt out what he did that awful night he came to dinner at the Majestic. It was never discussed. Years passed and my sisters and I accepted that whatever had happened between Grandpa and our mother was so awful that there would never be another attempt at reconciliation, and there never was.

By chance, we learned the truth from Jeannie, Dad's youngest sister, years later when we were young adults. She had assumed we knew what had caused this deep rift in our family.

To my utter astonishment, Jeannie told me I was not the eldest child in my family as I had always presumed. Three years before I was born, my mother had given birth to a boy, their true first-born. When he was seven months old, he became violently ill with a stomach flu and died a few days later.

Jeannie vividly remembered how her family had just sat down for dinner that night when my distraught parents, white-faced and trembling, stumbled into their house to deliver the shattering news. Jeannie had burst into tears and Grandma Yetta rushed over to hug them close.

Stoically, Wolf sat in his place at the table unmoving, offering nothing. Suddenly, he erupted into a violent rage aimed at my mother. "You killed my grandson," he screamed over and over again, hammering the table with his fists. Dad led his wife, whimpering, away from the house. Jeannie, a young girl at the time, sat horror stricken as the scene played out.

When I was born a couple years later, the fence had been tenuously mended. Terrible things had been said by Wolf, all unforgivable, yet my parents forgave him. When I was hospitalized that winter with a ruptured appendix, Wolf's rage toward my mother resurfaced with the same accusations and the same recriminations. That long ago dinner at the Majestic had been an effort to reconcile the family.

As my aunt finished her loathsome tale, an unbidden memory suddenly surfaced of a particular instance I had witnessed years ago as a young teenager, yet had not understood at the time. I had found my mother, bent over, sitting alone in her darkened bedroom. Tears slid unbridled down her cheeks. She brought a hand-painted photograph to her lips and kissed the photograph gently. I caught a glimpse of a baby with blonde hair smiling a sweet, lopsided grin.

Incredibly, I saw my father's brilliant blue eyes looking out at me.

9
Little Ballerina

Despite being hidden in the closet shadows with its base now hopelessly lopsided, once I turned the key to the music box and "Dance, Ballerina, Dance" played and the miniature ballerina spun about, I knew who had left it at the Majestic: our once-upon-a-time resident ballerina.

Maya Petrov, a classically trained ballerina, had joined her parents, Rose and Henry, for part of their vacation at our cottage while her dance studio took a summer break. Just because she couldn't take classes did not mean Maya allowed her body to relax, however. Occasionally I would catch a glimpse of her perfecting different ballet positions, arching her back, lifting her foot high, spreading her knees wide, slender arms arched over her head. She practiced in a far corner of the Majestic's wraparound porch using the railing as a barre a couple hours each day.

Maya dressed for what she had come to do. She wore a leotard, matching slippers, and her black hair was pulled taut into a bun even though no one was there to see her as she moved through her routine.

Although she was here at a beach to enjoy herself, she neither sunbathed nor swam. Outdoor activities were forbidden all year round for a ballerina. When she did venture out, it was usually late afternoon and she would wear dark, oversized sunglasses, a wide-brimmed hat and pale, voluminous dresses with long sleeves to protect her body. Ballerinas had pearly white skin; a suntan was out of the question. She could never relax like a normal teenager, swimming in the surf, lying on a beach, eating whatever she wanted. Maya lived by a rigid code.

That she was the offspring of Rose and Henry Petrov was astonishing to one and all, most of all to her parents, who doted on her. We could tell that from the moment their daughter arrived, they not only loved her but were in awe of her.

Henry Petrov was a postman, Rose a stenographer, and they lived in a small, two-bedroom apartment outside of Toronto. From the photos they carried of her practicing in her bedroom, we could tell they had done everything to help her achieve her dream, going so far as to install a barre and mirrors in her bedroom. I noticed from the photos that the colorful trappings of a teenager were missing in her room. Her twin bed, covered with a plain tailored spread was pressed tight against the opposite wall along with a small dresser. It seemed to me that her room was monastic, housing a miniature studio, that incidentally included a place to sleep. But the Petrovs were proud they had done this for her.

Born Molly, Maya had legally changed her name a few years ago, since an aspiring ballerina whose dancing was becoming recognized needed a more artistic name. She had been offered an opportunity to audition for a prestigious ballet troupe in Canada at the end of August. Maya would spend the last ten days of her parents' vacation rehearsing in the city.

Besides her parents, everyone at the cottage was very excited for Maya. Many of the people staying with us had never been to a live ballet and here was a near professional ballerina staying at the same summer home they were at. Everyone wanted desperately to see her dance, so Maya agreed to a short performance to take place in the backyard of the Majestic.

Dad installed a few strings of outdoor lights behind the patio. The summer guests helped him set up folding lawn chairs and picnic benches about the yard, and families spread blankets on the grass. The concrete patio behind the cottage would become Maya's makeshift stage and Mr. Petrov would operate his portable record player and co-ordinate the music. Dad borrowed two torchiere lamps from our living room and set votive candles and lanterns up in the backyard. A full moon rose above us casting its light. Even though the set-up was primitive, Maya agreed it was fine, no problem.

And so, on a warm Saturday night toward the end of July, as blackness of night crept over the backyard, our humble surroundings vanished. Maya stepped daintily onto the grass. She was dressed in a white, knee-length tutu, hair knotted tight in a bun, ribbon-laced slippers on her feet. She smiled and gracefully bowed to her audience.

Slowly she began to sway to the strains of Tchaikovsky's *Swan Lake*. Mesmerized, we watched as her movements became as one with the music. Maya captivated us with an excerpt of Prokofiev's *Cinderella* and then one of Aurora gleaned from *Sleeping Beauty*. I was barely able to breathe, so fearful was I that the moment would shatter and hurl me away from this world of grace.

The most haunting ballet was saved for last: *Giselle*. Mournful sounds mingled with Maya's delicate movements as she danced with an unseen ensemble of sylph-like spirits, abandoned brides known as the Willies. Miraculously, the Willies had brought Giselle, a peasant girl, back to life after she died of a broken heart caused by her unfaithful lover, Albrecht. The Willies would punish Albrecht by forcing him to dance with all the Willies until he died of exhaustion. In the beginning, Giselle desperately wanted her revenge, but she relented and interceded to prevent him dying in this cruel way as she loved him still. We sat there spellbound as the story unfolded.

There were no breathtaking sets of eerie forest landscapes where the Willies first appeared, no wisps of smoke to set the mood. There was no real stage, no professional lighting; there were no accomplished musicians. Maya simply danced with passion to the scratchy music emanating from the record player her father manned.

We, her unsophisticated audience sat bewitched, tears pooling in our eyes, overwhelmed by this young dancer's ability to recreate the haunting tale with such beauty and delicacy. When her performance ended, Dad rushed up to hand her a bouquet of flowers. Someone in the audience shouted, "Bravo! Bravo!" The rest of us clapped until our hands were red and jumped up from our seats in her honor. Maya held the flowers in her arms as she bowed for us.

After that memorable weekend, she returned to the city. The auditions for the ballet company were being held soon, and Maya planned on training very hard to prepare herself for this wonderful opportunity. She looked pale and tired when she left, but it was understandable because of her strenuous schedule.

Rose would lament, "I wish she wouldn't work so hard. There's more to life than dancing."

Henry would answer with sad resignation, "But dance is her life."

Two weeks later she came back to the Majestic to help her parents pack for their return home. Everyone was shocked at her appearance. Maya looked gaunt and noticeably thinner. She tried to explain her changed appearance, blaming it on the intensity of her routine, assuring everyone she was fine.

Once July ended, it seemed as if August galloped away at an accelerated pace and suddenly it was time to close the cottage for another year. We hadn't heard from the Petrovs about Maya's audition, so in early September Dad called them in Toronto to see how things had gone. The news was not good. Maya had allowed herself to get so thin and worn down, she was physically unable to audition. Now depressed and devastated about her lost opportunity, she lay in bed lethargic, barely eating. Maya no longer danced, and music no longer filled their home in Toronto.

There were always some special people that became an integral part of our lives as they briefly passed through the Majestic. It never became any easier to accept that they could simply disappear as quickly as they had come. The Petrovs never returned for another stay with us.

Finding Maya's music box all these years later evoked bittersweet memories for me. If I close my eyes very tightly, I can still hear the tinny music emanating from Henry's ancient phonograph player. I can envision Maya's sculpted arms gracefully extended above her head, her feet in her silk slippers, set to perform. A moment later she is dancing with abandon, leaping high, caught in the moonlight, surrounded by flickering candles and a mesmerized audience, witnessing her debut at the Majestic with such joy.

10
The Cherished Tree

The sour cherry tree grew in Mr. Oliver's yard close to the Majestic's property line. Over time, the pretty tree with its delicate pink flowers had grown larger and its overladen branches crept over the flimsy fence between us. When we visited the cottage every June weekend, we could see the mature tree was producing more cherries than it had ever before.

As the branches became heavier and weighted down with fruit, the cherries began dropping into our back yard. They were at their peak, so ready for easy eating. My sisters and I grabbed them as soon as they fell from the lower hanging branches, rinsed them under the garden hose and gulped them down quickly.

Mother said, "This is ridiculous! Why wait until the cherries actually drop to the ground. We'll just pick the ones on our side of the tree before they land."

It certainly made sense.

Mr. Oliver, whom everyone called Big Ollie, had been lying on his hammock drinking a beer when he saw us doing just that. Huffing and puffing his way over to where we were, he grumbled, "What's going on here? Just what the hell do you think you girls are doing?" Myrna was precariously balanced on a wicker stool plucking the cherries and tossing them into a basket. His scowling face startled her so badly, she fell to the ground and then ran crying back to the house.

Mother strode resolutely into the backyard to see what was going on.

She could hear Big Ollie on the other side of the fence screaming at Linda and me. "You all get away from this here tree. You brats have no right stealing my cherries. If you know what's good for you, you'll stay away." He shook his left hand at us furiously as his other still tightly gripped the beer. Big Ollie's face was flushed, his eyes were narrowed into slits, and perspiration streaked his forehead.

"Here we have a problem, Ollie," Mother shouted to him. "You're scaring my children with your shenanigans. What the heck's the matter with you?" she demanded.

"What's the matter with me," he growled, "you have one helluva nerve. I own this tree and your girls have no right to help themselves to my cherries. They're thieves, and you'd be better off punishing them instead of bawling me out."

"Whatever comes over that fence is my property," the mistress of the Majestic informed him. She stooped down to gather up some of the cherries that Myrna had dropped and threw them back into the basket. Big Ollie stared at our mother in slack-jawed rage.

The large man clutched the trunk of the tree and shook it furiously. "You are not to take my cherries without my permission," he shrieked as even more cherries dropped off the tree. "I'm comin' over there right now to pluck them off before you rob me blind. They're mine."

"You'd better think twice, Ollie," Mother warned. "There are laws against coming on someone else's property uninvited. It's called trespassing."

"We'll just see about that," he sputtered, but Ollie did not come into our yard during those June weekends when we were there getting the cottage ready for summer. Cherries that had fallen to our side during our absences still lay on the ground.

Mother tended to be very stingy about the cherries she personally gathered but there was an ulterior motive. She'd rinse the cherries, remove their stems, and then fill a large vat with enough water to cover the fruit. We leaned in closer to watch as she added a couple envelopes of yeast, a cup of sugar, and a glass or two of Canadian whiskey. She gently stirred it with a wooden spoon and covered her concoction with cheesecloth. "It's resting," Mother said.

At first this combination looked just like what it was: cherries awash in a sea of liquids. However, within a day or so, we'd hear a weird gurgle or a hiccup erupt from within as the ingredients began to get acquainted with one another. The vat remained on the kitchen counter as the contents mingled and grew more potent daily. Whenever Mother added more fruit, she added bit more alcohol, too. She was in the process of brewing a potent cherry liqueur Dad nicknamed *Ida's Moonshine*.

Whenever Ollie noticed any of us gathering cherries, he would stride angrily over to the fence and unleash his obvious displeasure. As time went on, my sisters and I became accustomed to his bluster and would temporarily remove ourselves until he stopped battering the tree about and stumbled back to his hammock. If Mother heard him shouting and cussing, she'd always rush out of the cottage to remind him, "We're entitled to anything that lands on our property."

Dad did not approve of what was happening. "Cherries are not that expensive and this argument with Ollie isn't worth the aggravation."

"It's the principle," Mother insisted, but she never expanded on what the principle was exactly.

Dad would have preferred to have no part in this ongoing feud, but unfortunately Ollie noticed him out in the backyard one day and snarled, "You should do something about that wife of yours. She and your wild kids just keep helping themselves to my cherry tree."

"Ollie, I don't even see you picking the cherries up on your own side," Dad said. "They are all over your backyard just rotting. So what's the big deal if my wife picks the ones that land on our side? Who does it hurt?"

"Those are my cherries," said Big Ollie, his face growing red and his voice rising, "and I can do anything or nothing with them if I choose. I don't have to answer to you."

"This is a big fuss over nothing," said Dad, dismissing him with a wave of his hand. "If it bothers you that much, why don't you just replant the tree somewhere else on your lot? You've got plenty of room."

Ollie barked at him "Like a tree is so easy to move."

Meanwhile, the cherries that had been soaking continuously for a couple of weeks had undergone a transformation. They had split open and fermented. Their juice had combined with the other potent ingredients to produced a burnished, amber-colored liquid that emitted a pleasant earthy aroma, now thick and syrupy. Mother had skimmed away the liquored up cherries and strained them through cheesecloth until the liquid was clear.

After one last sampling, Mother declared her mishmash done. She poured it into jelly jars and announced that it was finally ready for human consumption.

That evening after dinner, my parents filled cordial glasses with the homemade brew and settled themselves outside on the porch to savor Mother's hooch.

"This is the best you have ever made," Dad exalted. "Fit for a king," he announced as he settled back in his chair.

"Ha," she laughed. "You mean fit for a queen, my dear," and they both chuckled.

"You know," Dad mused, "We've had our share of problems with

Ollie from day one about the cherries, but I think if we gave him a bit of this stuff, it might go a long way toward making peace with him. What do you say?"

Mother, possibly a little more mellow than usual, agreed. "Sure, let bygones be bygones!"

Our surly neighbor was quite surprised to find Dad at his doorway bringing him a gift. Ollie took a swig from the jar, paused and then took another even longer one. "Pretty damned good stuff," he admitted begrudgingly.

"Glad you like it," Dad smiled.

Ollie said solemnly, "I'm pretty sure I won't be drinking anything quite this fine too soon again. Thank the missus."

When Dad came home, he gave Mother a glowing account of how well his visit went. "The man really appreciated that firewater you sent him." He laughed. "I think everything's going to be okay between us now."

It wasn't noticeable at first, but the leaves on the cherry tree slowly became dry and brittle. Many of the leaves developed dark spots and fell from their branches. Cherries that still clung looked shriveled. The tree was no longer thriving. Dad saw deep slashes on the roots of the tree and on its trunk, probably made with an axe. Not too far away lay a discarded can of weed killer. Ollie had murdered his own tree.

The cherry tree he savaged was neither cut down nor removed. It remained a blackened symbol of revenge for him to savor from his hammock. It was a sad reminder to my sisters and me of the man's bile. We all felt badly about this carnage except for our indomitable mother.

"Who cares," she scoffed, flinging her arms wide. "No great loss. I always thought his cherries tasted way too bitter anyway."

11
Miz Delly

It was one of her iron-clad rules. My mother, proprietress of the Majestic, absolutely did not rent to families with very young children. But then along came the Delaganos. Their daughter, Kimberly, was under a year old and they wanted to rent one of our two cabins for the month of July. This family was so likable that Mother found herself unable to deny them and arrangements were finalized. Mr. Delagano planned to come out only on weekends, but his wife and child would be there the rest of the time to enjoy the beach.

That first morning in early July, Mrs. Delgono had laid a blanket outside on the grass. Baby Kimmy was happily crawling everywhere but on the blanket. "Come here you little devil," her mom laughed as she scooped her up. "Where do you think you are going?"

My nine-year-old sister Myrna, three-year-old Linda, and I had been silently observing them. They looked as if they were having so much fun. Mrs. Delegano beckoned us over and whispered to Kimmy, "Look who's come over to visit."

"Hi, Missus" I said and futilely attempted to pronounce her last name.

She chuckled, "How about you just call me Miz Delly."

Unexpectedly, she clutched us to her in an enormous bear hug. I knew our parents loved us, but they weren't demonstrative. Being hugged so fiercely was a brand-new experience for us and it felt nice.

We cuddled Kimmy on our laps while she squirmed and laughed. She crawled all over the grass with my sisters and me following her. Kimmy would turn her head to see if we were still behind her, and then dissolve in giggles. We played with her, sang to her, recited nursery rhymes, and cuddled her as she squirmed mischievously in our arms.

"What are you bothering Mrs. Delagano for?" Mother scolded us at lunchtime. "The woman's busy enough just taking care of her baby without you all pestering her."

I shook my head. "No, it's not like that. Miz Delly invited us."

Mother scoffed, "She's just being polite. You're eleven now and should know better. Just leave her alone."

We quickly discovered Miz Delly was a very difficult person to just leave alone. The next morning she asked Mother if we could go to the beach with her and it was okayed. Our oversized wood wagon was loaded with blankets, towels, food, baby Kimmy, plus our baby sister, Linda. Myrna and I curled our smaller fingers over Miz Delly's to help her pull the wagon, and off we went.

The cart had to be left on the boardwalk near the entrance to the beach, since it was impossible to push it across the soft sand. It took several trips for us just to get everything down to the shoreline, but finally Miz Delly spread out the beach blankets and we settled in.

Lovingly, she held Kimmy in her arms as she spread tanning lotion over all the exposed parts of her baby, murmuring endearments as she did. Every gesture, caress, each word, was a confirmation of the love she felt for her daughter. My sister Myrna and I clasped hands and locked eyes in wonder. We were witnessing a moment of enormous tenderness that left us feeling deprived yet unable to articulate the reason. As quickly as the moment came it vanished, and Miz Delly smoothed lotion over us, too.

Myrna and I tried to teach the little ones how to float while we held their small bodies above the waves. We toted pails of water over to where they were digging in the sand, taught them to roll a beach ball to one another, and stepped in when they wanted the same toy. After lunch, we all spread out on the blankets to rest and even though no one ever felt tired, we dozed.

Miz Delly always asked Mother's permission for us to accompany her to the beach before going. Despite Miz Delly giving our hard-working mother a welcomed break, her attitude toward Miz Delly was ambivalent. While grateful, she seemed mildly irritated that Miz Delly spent so much more time with her children than she was able to.

There was such a pleasant symmetry to our days that summer. It was easy to lose track of time and suddenly it was the twenty-sixth of July. When we realized Miz Delly would be gone within the week, Myrna and I lamented about how much we were going to miss her. "Sweeties, don't worry." She grinned as she held up her right hand. "I solemnly promise to be back next year and every year thereafter. If I stayed too long, we'd run out of fun things to do." As if that could ever happen, I thought, brushing away a tear.

On one of her last days with us, we spent the day at the beach as usual. We nestled into our favorite spot, splashed about in warm waters, and sculpted magnificent sand castles. Miz Delly treated us for ice cream cones, cold and dripping under the hot sun. We chuckled at baby Kimmy's facial expressions, first of distaste, then of wonder as she discovered she liked this strange, icy food. We spotted the *Canadiana* steamship approaching Crystal Beach as it did every day, just a bit before four o'clock in the afternoon. This typically would have been our cue to start for home, but no one wanted to leave. It was such an idyllic day.

Kimmy nodded off then, as did the rest of us. Stretched out, relaxed and sated, we snoozed under the warm sun. Miz Delly woke with a start. It was five-thirty in the afternoon, and she said my sisters and I were going to be late for dinner. Hurriedly we packed our things and began trudging toward the boardwalk. Most people had already left and the beach was deserted.

Suddenly I shrieked and fell to the sand screaming in pain. I had just stepped on a lit cigarette. In seconds, everything changed. Instead of dwelling in the delightful afterglow of another magnificent day, Miz Delly found herself alone and scared. She was staring across a desolate beach surrounded by four sobbing children, all looking to her for comfort she wasn't sure she could provide.

Miz Delly offered her elbow to me for support, and I clung tenaciously to that small woman as she struggled to haul me up to the boardwalk while carrying Kimmy in her arms. Our possessions were left in disarray, abandoned where they lay, suddenly very unimportant.

Miz Delly settled me in the wagon, placing an unhappy Kimmy between my legs. Piteously sobbing, the little girl raised her chubby arms to be picked up. Time and time again, she was firmly returned back into the wagon by a resolute Miz Delly.

Linda was irate that she had been ousted from the wagon. Whimpering, she plunked herself down on the sidewalk and refused to walk any further. Only when we continued without her, would she rush to catch up with us. Baby Kimmy, railing at the injustice of having to share her ride with a larger person, never ceased wailing. Slowly Miz Delly made the hellish trek back to the Majestic barely able to tow our overburdened caravan back home.

Bedlam reigned as soon as we entered the Majestic and Mother saw me limping. "It was my fault," I hastily explained. "I should have looked where I was going." Mother applied salve to the burn, bandaged it, gave me aspirin and left me in the darkened bedroom to rest with a wet cloth on my forehead.

Although my door was shut, I could hear them clearly. Mother admonished Miz Delly. "Why didn't you insist she wear her sandals on the hot sand? People toss lit cigarettes on the beach all the time."

"I'm so very sorry about this." Miz Delly pleaded for understanding. "The sand had cooled by then and we were in a hurry to get home." Her voice dropped to a whisper. "After stepping on that cigarette, she could barely walk."

I could hear Miz Delly's sweet voice breaking. "I love your girls and would never do anything to hurt them."

"Yet you did," Mother said.

Like a mantra, I kept repeating to myself, "It was only an accident, it was only an accident," and fell asleep hypnotized by my own words.

Around eight o'clock that night, I awoke and hobbled over to the kitchen table. Mother gently kissed my cheek, and asked how I was feeling, then went about preparing a snack for me since I had slept right through supper. I guessed the argument that had raged earlier had been resolved. Everything was very calm and quiet.

Myrna, eyes red and swollen, joined me in the kitchen. Assuming I was the reason for her distress, I lightheartedly said, "It hardly hurts now. Don't worry, I'm fine."

Myrna shouted, "It's not you I'm crying about. It's Miz Delly. She called her husband from the drugstore and he came and took her and Kimmy back to Buffalo."

It had never occurred to me that this would happen, but then again, how could it not? Even though Mother was very protective of us, was it possible that she was also jealous of Miz Delly, too? Despite her solemn promise of many more splendid summers to come, Miz Delly was gone. With sad certainty, I knew that kindly woman would never again vacation at the Majestic.

My sister's expectations and mine had been for a much more joyful ending to this tale. We had envisioned summer after magical summer together for years to come. As easily as Miz Delly entered our lives, she slipped away. Even though this "passing through the Majestic" happened often, it never, ever became easier for us to accept, especially when people exited our lives so abruptly.

12
A Change Of Scenery

It was springtime, late April, and we were once again at the Majestic Cottage in Canada for our annual inspection and initial cleanup to ready it for summer. Even before we got there, Mom and Dad had decided that the kitchens and adjoining dining room were starting to look dingy. Dad intended to brighten the rooms with a fresh coat of paint before our cottage opened in late June.

The color of the walls was a dull green-gray. My mother said she wanted something with more pizazz, something lighter that would make the rooms look larger than they were. We came armed that day with all kinds of paint swatches to determine which color to choose. Mother loved lavender but that was hardly suitable for a kitchen. Her second choice was a cerulean blue. We set the sample against the wall, and it was immediately apparent that it was too vibrant a color for that kitchen, so out of sync with our old-fashioned appliances and rustic furniture. Although my sisters and I loved pink, we knew it wouldn't make the cut.

Beige was considered too dull and yellow, too glaring. Dad said, "I actually like the green we have. Even if we use the same shade, it would still be fresh and new."

My mother was incredulous. "What's the point of even painting the rooms at all if it's going to look exactly the same? I want something new and different," she insisted. "The Majestic is a vacation destination after all," she expounded. After thinking about it a while, her hand held against her chin, she brightened and said, "How about cantaloupe?"

My first thought was that she was referring to pre-sliced melon possibly brought from Buffalo to snack on, but she wasn't. "What do you all think about painting the kitchen the color of the inside of a cantaloupe?" she asked. We didn't even have a sample swatch of that color to hold against the wall to imagine how that would look, but the more Mother talked up the color, that it was bright, it was different, the more appealing it became. Our family began to embrace the idea of a light orange color transforming this drab, gloomy area.

The following weekend, Dad labored to finish the paint job by Sunday, and when it was done, we stared in awe. Indeed, it felt exactly like being in the center of a ripe cantaloupe, something most people surely had never experienced. I thought to myself, this will take some getting used to, but Mother was overjoyed and cried out, "This is just exactly what I wanted it to look like! Harry, you did a beautiful job. Thank you! Thank you." She rushed over and gave him a big kiss on the cheek.

And so, April turned to May, and on to June. No one was in the kitchen that much during those months, so we were hardly aware of the color change once we got accustomed to it. Mother rarely cooked when we were in the draconian regimen of getting the cottage cleaned up and spiffy for the new season. We would scarf down our cold sandwiches in the back yard, rushing because there was always something that needed doing inside the cottage. The Majestic was a stern overseer.

Mother bought a roll of pale orange oilcloth to complement the new wall color, carefully trimming it to fit the various sizes of tables in the kitchen and dining room. She filled clear glass vases with artificial marigolds and green leaves. The room felt cozy and very warm. Our cantaloupe kitchen was ready for its debut.

We opened up the cottage for guests the last week of June when school ended. We perked along quite nicely during the first weeks of July, but then, my parents noticed a strange phenomenon. Our occupants were easily irritated, testier and more short-tempered over trifling matters than ever. We had more mishaps in the kitchen and the first aid kit was suddenly needed more often. Something was simply not right. No one could figure out what was off and why our guests were more fidgety than usual. Everything was exactly as it had been the year before except for one thing: the brightly colored kitchen and dining areas.

We hadn't a clue about how color could affect mood, but it soon became painfully apparent that people aren't meant to cook their vittles and eat them in the center of a cantaloupe on a warm summer day. The kitchen and dining areas felt physically hotter than any other part of the cottage despite the constant lake breezes wafting through the open windows.

Our guests stayed from Sunday to Sunday. It became apparent by the time the weekend came, our people were more stressed than when they had first arrived and seemingly more anxious to leave. The whimsical aspect of having a cantaloupe-colored kitchen had completely worn away. Ordinarily once a problem of this magnitude was identified, my father would have promptly remedied it. Hastily, he would have repainted those rooms in a day or two, but those vital areas simply could not be exempted from use during our busiest weeks of the summer.

Mother attempted to minimize the impact of the walls by exchanging the pale orange tablecloths with plain white ones. She tossed out the marigolds and replaced them with artificial white lily flowers, surrounded with many green stems and leaves. She purchased a set of white dishes with lemon-colored borders and stowed away our more vibrant pieces. Dad hung up a few fern planters to make the room seem more outdoorsy. Ways had to be found to neutralize the situation before the cantaloupe-tinted rooms doomed the Majestic's popularity.

Another solution was to lessen the use of a kitchen that contributed to such frenzied behavior. Dad bought a couple of barbecue grills, charcoal, spatulas, grill forks and tongs. He began to use the equipment to cook delicious food in the backyard, hopefully to encourage others to do the same. He also bought a new picnic table with seating for twelve to lure people outside of the cottage. Then he tacked up a blackboard on a tree for folks to reserve grilling time slots, using a chalk stick on weekends. The sign-up slate was already filled with reservations by noon. The women found they loved the idea that their men were busy charbroiling hot dogs or hamburgers while all they had to do was pop open bags of chips and serve up pickles and soda.

I always thought that our backyard was the most pleasant of places to be. Lush hedges cradled the borders of our property, insulating us from the harshness of the outside world. The summer flowers were now in full bloom, at their most brilliant and most fragrant. Lake breezes urged the wood chimes into soft melodic musical tones. Dad had strung strings of outdoor light bulbs about the patio that flickered on and off. So humdrum, so ordinary during the day, the backyard became entrancing after dusk.

Our cottage guests lingered long after they finished eating. They watched the sun slowly relinquish the day, as the coals in the grills turned to red embers before dissolving into ash. They talked on and on forever. There existed a camaraderie not apparent at any other time. The next morning no one really remembered what topics they had even touched upon, or the many conversations, yet it seemed only right that they congregate together there until all light was extinguished and the night was tucked in properly before they returned inside for bedtime.

We were the first boarding house to allow outdoor grilling. The chaotic interior of the cottage encouraged my parents to make the backyard an oasis, so much more inviting and accessible. The season ended on a triumphant note, and we happily shuttered the Majestic for another year.

The following spring Dad was eager to restore our kitchen and dining room to a more muted palette such as we had lived with in the past. My mother acquiesced to the idea that these rooms should be repainted the original green-gray color that had been on the walls probably forever. It was familiar and soothing, a safe choice that had served us well.

I knew, though, that my mother would never again allow the green-gray walls in the Majestic. That dull, boring color, so devoid of pizazz, would remain forever on the hardware store's shelves collecting dust. Luckily, while browsing one day, Mother had come upon an apple green paint she liked quite a bit better. Almost all of us agreed that it was far more suitable for a holiday destination on the sandy shores of Crystal Beach.

"I can't fight all of you," Dad sighed, as he paid for the apple green paint.

13
The Contest

Mother slammed the front door so forcefully the cottage vibrated from the impact. She was in an angry huff, and of course, we all knew why. Our parents had just returned from the annual Crestwood Bake-off, held the last week of July at the Crestwood Hotel near Niagara Falls. The event attracted people from nearby towns and hamlets up and down the Canadian shore, not far from where we spent our summers at the Majestic.

She had won no prize, not even a mention for this year's entry, an apricot cobbler infused with orange liqueur. "I really thought this was my best dessert ever," she lamented, "especially with my special touch, the orange liqueur.

Mother didn't take this competition lightly. After one contest ended, she immediately began an intense search for a memorable dessert that would catapult her into the coveted winner's circle. Our family was the beneficiary of her efforts, forming a willing taste-test panel of the tantalizing baked goods brought forth from the oven all winter long because of her intense determination to win this contest.

One afternoon, she and my sister Myrna were shopping in a large grocery store and noticed a group of people congregated near the baking supply aisle. They wandered over to see what had piqued so much interest. It was a product called Ultamonte flour. "The purity of our flour assures the baker of superior results. I guarantee it," the spokeswoman asserted and passed out samples of a Swedish Tea Cake that had been prepared earlier. The onlookers all commented on how good the tea cake was, how delicate, how outstanding.

Smiling, the spokeswoman announced that anyone who purchased a five-pound bag of flour would receive the Ultamonte Pantry Flour Recipe booklet as a complimentary gift. Inside were illustrations on how to prepare their company's baked goods, including the remarkable Swedish Tea Ring. Our mother was one of the first to scurry up to the sales counter to make a purchase. "I'm going to make that cake for my bridge club and see how they like it," she announced. Knowing our mother, we knew that the women she played bridge with were not her choice audience. She had something else up her sleeve.

Mother hadn't the slightest idea how labor intensive it was going to be to recreate this delicacy. The first step was the preparation of a yeast dough. Once all the ingredients were mixed, she kneaded the unwieldy mass into a ball, greased it lightly, covered it with a tea cloth, then, as advised by the instructions, left it to rise until it doubled in volume.

She then rolled out the dough on a floured board. She spread the nut- filled, cinnamon sugar mix over the dough, folding it up jelly roll style to form a circular ring. Mother pinched the corners together and then allowed the dough to rise once more before she baked it. When the aromatic tea cake emerged from the oven, it not only smelled delicious, but had expanded even more in size. This Swedish Tea Ring was big enough to serve sixteen delicious pieces. When completely cooled, Mother drizzled a vanilla glaze over the entire cake.

This undertaking had consumed Mother's entire morning. Despite the many phases involved in her project, she was delighted with the outcome. "It looks exactly like the tea ring in the store," she extolled. The friends who attended the April bridge club meet were as impressed as Mother had been the first time she had tasted the Swedish Tea Cake. When questioned about the makings of this dessert, she modestly admitted that it was an old family recipe she'd made countless times before.

After the bridge group's success, Mother exclaimed "This cake could be a winner! I'm definitely going to bake it for the Crestwood contest, exactly as the instructions read without any changes," she announced excitedly after the bridge players left. "After all," she reasoned, "how can I improve on something that's already perfect?"

June and early July were hectic months for Mother as proprietress of the Majestic, and that year was an exceptionally busy one because the cottage was constantly filled to capacity. The days were long and tiring. As June slipped into July, Mother's enthusiasm for preparing the tea ring for the bake-off slackened whenever she recalled the complicated, laborious process involved. Although confident that that cake was a strong contender, she was far less enthusiastic than earlier in the season about devoting half a day to its construction. "Maybe this year," she said, "I won't be a contestant." Ten year old Myrna solved the problem easily. "Don't worry," she said, "I'll be happy to make it."

One of Crestwood's rules for the bake-off was that only adults were permitted to enter. I think Mother reconciled any misgivings she might have had with the rationale that she had never been recognized by the judges for past endeavors, so what difference did it make, if just this one time, she didn't do the baking herself? After all, there was no guarantee the cake would even be acknowledged. Certainly, she had been wrong in the past, hoping that what she had submitted was worthy of recognition.

My sister began preparing the dessert before dawn, long before anyone was awake at the cottage. It emerged from the oven as flawless as Mother's, but it didn't look quite like the original cake that Mother had made for her bridge party. Myrna had gotten creative and added a bit of English marmalade to the filling, substituted a lemon glaze for the topping and sprinkled shredded almonds over everything. When Mother saw what Myrna had done, she was appalled. Even though the changes might have been considered subtle, the cake emerged from the oven even larger than it had been before because of the additional frosting, filling, and toppings. It simply wasn't what Mother had expected Myrna to do and there was no time to rebake it. This mutated Swedish Tea Cake would be entered into the competition as it was, and Mother would have to claim it as her own.

Dad had brought the family car up for the weekend for this supposedly special occasion, but the mood in the car was somber as we drove to the Crestwood Hotel. Myrna sat quietly in the corner of the car, her hand on her mouth as if she blamed herself for not being able to leave well enough alone.

"We're all getting too worked up over this contest," Dad reminded everyone. "Let's all settle down and remember it's not an event that's going to change anybody's life that much. All I know for sure is that the cake smells absolutely scrumptious, and I can't wait to eat a piece of it. Now let's all try to relax a bit."

The Crestview Hotel had a substantial ballroom set up for this annual event. Garlands of flowers and potted plants decorated the room. Soft music played. White folding chairs had been arranged into rows and put before the podium. Nearby, the exhibition tables had been set up and were covered with the baked goods offered for viewing. While desserts were displayed over white doilies on cake plates and stands, the Swedish Tea Cake, already gargantuan in size, was set upon a towering pedestal.

Within these pleasant surroundings, everyone felt anticipation and excitement as they waited for the tastings to begin. "I wish I was home," Mother moaned.

The three judges glided from one dessert to the next, delicately nibbling teensy forkfuls of each with eyes closed, while scribbling cryptic notes on the small pads they carried. Participants in the contest carefully watched the stoic judges, hoping to glean some indication of what they were thinking, but to no avail. A pre-arranged intermission gave the judges time to make their difficult decisions.

When the lights finally blinked on and off to signal that the selections had been made, people quickly returned to their seats. With fanfare, one by one, the winning entries were announced. The lovely mocha cream puffs placed third and the decadent-looking caramel pecan pie won second. The elated winners rushed to the dais to receive praise for their ingenuity and skill.

Suddenly a hush fell over the Crestwood's Ballroom. Following a dramatic moment or two of silence, a drum roll heralded the announcement for the first-place winner. The head judge walked solemnly to the microphone. Finally, the moment everyone had been waiting for had arrived. The talented contestant who had won this high honor was announced to jubilant, thunderous applause and incredibly, that contestant was our mother. She stood up, smiled and walked regally up to the podium to accept the coveted award.

Everyone was jovial on the drive back home, especially Mother, who was giddy with happiness. Amidst all the jubilation surrounding this momentous achievement, it was entirely forgotten that Myrna had actually been the creator of that formidable cake, and it could never be acknowledged. Mother's trophy was left on display on the mantle of the Majestic.

That year marked the last time our mother ever entered the Crestwood's bake-off competition. The zealousness, the passion with which she had approached the event yearly, disappeared abruptly and never returned. Friends and acquaintances were convinced it was because she had nothing more to prove.

I think she finally accepted the fact that she could never really win it herself.

14
Like is in the Air

We met Clare, a woman in her late thirties, when she came out to the Majestic hoping to arrange a two-week stay for three people. When Mother pointed out that her bedrooms were much too small for that many adults, Clare said her brother was just a little five-year-old kid.

Now Mother wasn't born yesterday, and she knew that the little five-year-old boy was more likely Clare's son than her brother. She certainly had her faults, but I never saw Mother judge anyone on how they led their lives, a rarity in those times.

Clare brought her small family back from the park to meet the Majestic's proprietress, half expecting Mrs. Zarne to back out of their deal. Inwardly, Mother applauded Clare's pluckiness for keeping her child, even if she couldn't freely acknowledge him. Mother made up her mind that their little family would be our honored guests for as long as they were at the Majestic and would be treated with every courtesy.

Late Friday morning the trio—Clare, her mother, Lena, and the youngster, Jesse, arrived in Crystal Beach on a Greyhound Bus. They dragged their bags the two blocks to the Majestic. Once there, Lena shooed Clare out of the cottage so Clare could get in some fun-time.

It was an absolutely beautiful afternoon for Jesse and Clare to enjoy their first day on the beach. They had just set their blanket up near the shore, where a boy, about the same age as Jesse, waded in the water. He introduced himself as Danny.

"I'm here most every day with Anna," Danny said, pointing to his nanny, "but never on weekends because my dad hates the sun."

"How can anybody hate the sun?" Jesse asked in wonder. "Doesn't your mom like the sun either?"

"I don't know," Danny answered," I don't have a mom. She died when I was just a little baby."

Jesse said, "I don't have a dad, but I don't think he's dead."

Danny grabbed Jesse's hand and off they ran into the waves. The boys had bonded very quickly.

When it was time to leave for the day, Danny sadly announced that he probably wouldn't be back to the beach again until after the weekend because his dad avoided the sun. He assured Jesse he'd be back by Monday, and they set up a place to meet.

Shortly after Clare and Jesse reached the beach on Saturday afternoon, they were surprised to see Jesse's friend was already there with his dad. As soon as Danny spotted them, he dragged his father over to meet his new friends.

"Cliff, Danny's father, is a redhead and has very pale skin," Clare told us all when she returned that afternoon. "I have to tell you his dad was quite a sight when I first met him." Clare said with a chuckle. "He wore a long shirt with wrist-length sleeves, a big beach hat, enormous sun glasses and had white ointment spread all over his nose and cheeks, but he came out 'cause his son wanted him to meet Jesse. I think that says a lot about the man, don't you think?"

Sunday was another great beach day; the temperature reached the high eighties. Cliff and Danny spent the whole day with Jesse and Clare. It was nearing five o'clock in the afternoon when they left, only to make arrangements for Cliff and Danny to pick them up an hour later for an evening in the midway of the park. The boys just couldn't seem to get enough of one another.

That night, when Cliff drove to the Majestic, he knocked on the front door to pick up Jesse and Clare. She introduced him to all of us sitting out on the porch, including her mother, Lena.

"He's a nice man, that Cliff," Lena whispered to Clare before she left. "Do you like him?"

"Oh, Ma, "Clare laughed.

Cliff and Clare were of the same mind in thinking Crystal Beach was a better alternative for the summer than the city, even though both still worked in Buffalo. When he learned Clare had only a one-week vacation and wouldn't be out to the Majestic much during her second week, Cliff offered to remedy that. He suggested that he drive her to her Buffalo office each morning, and pick her up when she was through for a return ride to Crystal Beach.

"You'd have to start earlier than if you left directly from your apartment," Cliff warned, "but at least you'd have more time here." Clare was delighted.

Around seven o'clock nightly, Cliff and son would pop over to the Majestic and pick up Clare and Jesse for a fun night in the park, just two blocks away. Their suppers were Midway food: hamburgers, hot dogs, fries and custard cones. Often, they stopped at the Crystal Dance Hall located in the park. Lena would join them to treat the boys for a couple rides in the Midway while Cliff and Clare returned to the dance floor.

Clare felt that she had gained another week of vacation by coming out every night, thanks to Cliff. Sometimes they met for an early evening swim in the lake. The beach was far more deserted and the sun had begun its departure. Cliff joked, "I've found the perfect way to enjoy Crystal Beach."

"You're spending a lot of time with Cliff lately," Lena said. "So, what's what?"

"Cliff's a wonderful person, but way too fussy for me," Clare laughed. "He thinks things through a million times before he makes a decision and besides, he's ten years older than I am."

"And you're a spring chicken," Lena said.

On the last Saturday night of Clare's vacation, Cliff took her out for a fine dinner. "Grown up time," he joked. On Sunday afternoon, Clare, Lena and Jesse were returning to Buffalo in Cliff's car.

"We will definitely be back next summer, Mrs. Zarne," promised Clare as she hugged Mother goodbye. "It's been a great two weeks."

Mother asked mischievously, "Did you enjoy going out with Cliff last night?"

"I really like him, but we're way too different. Half the time, I don't even understand what Cliff is saying. I have to look words up in the dictionary, but even if I figure out what they mean, I still can't pronounce them. I guess he's more worldly than I am. He took me out for dinner last night and the whole menu was in French. I don't even know what I ate," Clare sighed. "He's a wonderful person, but he's not the man for me. I hope we'll always be good friends though."

"Did you enjoy the food at least?" Mother quipped.

By the time Fourth of July came the following year, we were again full at the Majestic and the usual chaos was once more upon us. My family wondered why Clare had not made her reservation for this summer, and we hoped she was all right.

My parents had just settled themselves out on the veranda after dinner one night, when a large station wagon with American plates pulled in front of the cottage. Two young boys we knew very well, Jesse and Danny, hopped from the back seat, then helped Jesse's grandmother, Lena, out. They rushed up our path toward our cottage, shouting greetings. Cliff gently guided Clare from the car and when she did appear, to our surprise, she was several months pregnant.

The newlyweds were very grateful to my Mother, convinced she was the catalyst for their happy outcome. This summer they would not be vacationing with us. Cliff had rented a private family cottage for them in Bay Beach.

Many times, people passed through the Majestic, then disappeared from our lives completely. Their fates were unfinished stories and we could only guess the outcome. This time we knew clearly that a happy ending had taken place.

The following summer we met their red-headed baby son, Billy.

"Who would have thought?" Lena smiled, as she held the little boy close. "Liking becomes loving and look what we have here."

"Who would have thought?" Mother grinned, as she kissed the baby's cheek.

15
Cecilia Comes Visiting

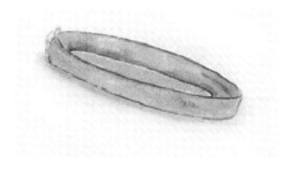

The summer was waning, and the Majestic was always a lot more quiet as September neared, almost as if it was declaring, "I served you well all these months and now I need a nap." It was always at this time that Miss Cecilia Finney came to vacation with us. Because Cecilia had been coming to us steadily for seven years during these uncrowded days, and because she was an ideal tenant, and because Mother liked her, Mother always reduced her rent.

Cecilia was a sweet-looking woman in her mid- forties when she first came to stay at the Majestic. Now she was fifty-two, and while her hair had turned white, there remained that pleasant smile on her face. The kindness in her eyes stayed unchanged from when she was a much younger woman. She was always very cordial to everyone at the cottage, and everyone was fond of her.

The year she turned fifty-two was the only time I could ever remembering Miss Cecilia ever looking sad. We were shocked to learn she was no longer employed at the real estate office she had worked for all her adult life. Miss Cecilia had really needed that job as she was a single woman supporting herself on a meager salary and had no living family. She was totally alone.

In years gone by, Cecilia had always been a rather reserved type of a person, but that year she stayed with us, there was a significant change. No longer the quiet little mouse, she had become very vocal about the injustices heaped upon her, by former employer, Howard Grantley of the Grantley's Real Estate.

"One can mince words and call it early retirement," she complained, "but it was terrible to get rid of me that way." Howard had fired her suddenly in April. While he had referred to her dismissal euphemistically as "retirement," she knew that wasn't what it really was. "For example," she expounded, "he had been most adamant that I leave as quickly and as quietly as possible."

"Because of your long years with this firm," Howard had told her stoically, "we'll let you finish up your week, but I want your keys to the office on my desk tonight before you leave. And for the rest of your time here, your only responsibility will be to answer the phones in the outside reception area."

"They threw me out like an old shoe," she lamented, "and I've always been the most reliable person there."

She continued. "'Cecilia dear,' they'd say. 'Would you bring me a cup of decaf? I like it caramel-colored and very, very hot. Cecilia dear, I need a water and make sure it's very, very cold.' I'd do their bidding willingly with a smile on my face. I wasn't hired as a waitress but was employed there to type important documents," she sighed, "as I told Howard repeatedly. Throughout those long days of servitude, I'd smile until I thought my face would crack and then long after the day was over, I'd go home to my small apartment almost too tired to eat. I gave my life to that company."

Surprisingly, Cecilia had found unexpected joy in the gold bracelet she had received as a farewell gift from some of the employees at Grantley's when she left. How Betsy, one of the clerks, had ever come up with that particular choice was a puzzlement to her. Cecilia thought it was a frivolous send-off, saying that a watch would have been far more appropriate, and even though she would never admit it, Cecilia told us how she really loved the bracelet. She secretly loved how it sparkled on her wrist, how it made her feel special, even pampered. Certainly, it was not something she would have ever bought for herself. Nightly, she polished it with a soft chamois cloth before storing it carefully away in its original black velvet box.

Unlike our other guests, Cecilia did not go to the beach. She never joined in the card games, nor went to movies or to the many church bingo games available in our small village. Celia didn't knit or cook or read anything other than the newspaper. Every evening, she went out for her solitary dinner. Mostly, Cecilia loved sitting out on the veranda making conversation with our other guests. She encouraged them to talk about their lives and listened raptly when they did. Wistfully, she'd ask them, "What's your secret for a happy life?" Bewildered, they'd laugh at her strange remark, never realizing how seriously that question was asked.

Mother was convinced Cecilia had been treated most unfairly by her employer. "Isn't it illegal for a business to give you such short notice?" she queried Cecilia. "Maybe it was age discrimination," she mused. "Had you ever thought to pursue your dismissal with Workmen's Comp?"

Cecilia shook her head dolefully. "No. No. I can't do that. The best thing for me to do is to try and put this all behind me," she muttered. "Anyway, it was all the fault of that fancy pen," she added softly. Mother shook her head in confusion.

One morning Cecilia came downstairs panicky. Had anyone seen her gold bracelet? It was missing and she always put it back in its black case when she went to sleep at night. It wasn't there now, nor any place else in her room that she had been tearing apart for the last hour. Everyone in the cottage joined in the search for the bracelet, looking behind furniture, peeking into nooks and crannies, in the washrooms, around her favorite chair, but it was futile. The bracelet was nowhere to be found. Cecilia seemed to be truly devastated and everyone at the cottage felt badly because they knew how much that lone piece of jewelry meant to her. It was her sole luxury.

Within the week, Polly, a summer guest at the cottage was alarmed to learn that her pearl earrings, surrounded by a ring of gold, had vanished. Ordinarily, she wore them all the time but thought she had left them inside her closed room before going to the beach. Once again everyone searched for missing jewelry. Mother said that she felt these were simply unfortunate, isolated incidences.

However, folded bills disappeared from one of the bathrooms; Mr. Herman had forgot them there after he was done showering. It was now glaringly apparent that among our guests existed a thief.

Dad installed locks on all the bedroom doors and each tenant received his own key. This was indeed a sad turn of events after all the years of operating the Majestic on an honor system. There were no further losses, but everything was now hunkered down, valuables safe and secure in locked rooms. The guests looked upon one another with suspicion and mistrust. A pall had fallen on the Majestic as we now knew that not everyone was who they appeared to be.

During the last week the Majestic was open, our place began to empty out. The last few days before Labor Day, the only tenant who remained was Cecilia. Before she left, she came downstairs to say goodbye to my mother and make tentative arrangements for her stay the following year.

Sunlight flickered off the gold rimmed earrings in Cecilia's ear lobes that Mother had never seen her wear. They looked identical to the ones she had always seen Polly wear. Looped around Cecilia's wrist was that adored retirement bracelet Cecilia claimed had gone missing.

"Cecilia," Mother said frowning, "I see you found your bracelet, but aren't those Polly's earrings you're wearing?"

"Yes," Cecilia answered boldly. "They certainly are. If people are careless with their things, it's not my job to protect them from themselves. The earrings were just lying around as if they were bought in a five and dime."

"Cecilia," Mother said diplomatically, "if you found Polly's earrings, you should return them to her immediately. I'll give you her phone number and you can let her know you have them."

Patting my mother's arm, Cecilia said soothingly, "No, no, I don't think I'm going to do anything of the sort, Mrs. Zarne. If people who have so much more than me don't treasure their stuff, it's really quite all right I keep their things. They'll always have so much more than I'll ever have anyway. Don't fret about it, my dear," she said smiling as she headed for the cottage doorway. "It's only fair that I get a piece of the pie too, like when I 'borrowed' Howard's special pen."

"Wait, Miss Cecelia," Mother called after her, now adopting a stern tone. "You stole those earrings and cash from my cottage? I won't stand for it. You have to make it up to those people."

Cecilia grinned benignly at my mother, "Don't worry so much, Missus," she chirped. "I won't tell if you don't." As she walked out of the cottage, she said, "See you next August!"

16
Game Of Chance

How I dreaded Friday nights because of the poker games that took place here in the Majestic's living room. From the moment the cards were dealt, the gamblers seemed to take over the entire cottage with their hoots and hollers when a pot was either won or lost. We kids at the cottage had to tiptoe past them to wend our way into the kitchen for a snack. The kitchen itself was barely maneuverable as it was crowded with the wives of the poker players playing pinochle. Everyone else at the cottage retired to their rooms early or fought off mosquitos on the backyard patio.

These old-time poker friends waited anxiously all week to meet here for the camaraderie rather than the few dollars won or loss. Halfway through the night, the guys would take a break for coffee and dessert and by eleven o'clock, they would all have left. Mother collected a small amount from each player and used that money for the playing cards and food she supplied. The guys took turns picking up beer but there was no hard liquor.

The stakes were five and ten cents and limited to only three raises to rein in excessive betting. Rarely did anyone lose more than ten dollars, yet that amount wasn't exactly "small potatoes" at a time when fifty cents could buy you a hot dog and a Coke. Every player hoped he would be the Big Winner of the night, yet each man knew he would have an enjoyable evening regardless of his financial outcome.

It was late August when Jake, one of the regulars, developed a terrible stomach ache early Wednesday morning. His brother drove him to a Buffalo hospital and Jake underwent gall bladder surgery that day. While all his buddies were happy he was now doing well, neither brother would be available for the Friday night game now less than forty-eight hours away.

Frantic appeals went out to substitutes but by the time Thursday night rolled around, the situation looked dismal. If they couldn't recruit two more card players, their poker game would be called off. I was sorry Jake was sick, but not unhappy about the possibility of their having to cancel the Friday gathering.

At the last minute, Joe asked Al, a co-worker to play, and he agreed to fill in. Al was a bookkeeper, a quiet analytical man who said he enjoyed an occasional game because it challenged his understanding of numbers. There were now six participants, and only one more person was needed to reach the criteria for the seven-handed poker game the men insisted upon.

Milly, a friend of my mother, had often mentioned that her husband Sam enjoyed poker, yet he only played occasionally. While Mother was fond of Milly, she had never taken a liking to Sam, but after talking it over with Dad, it was decided that because of the urgency of their plight, he should be invited. Sam agreed to fill in as number seven, and the Friday Night Poker game was now happily on.

Gamblers, being a rather suspicious lot, regularly wore what they felt was their lucky shirt or lucky socks to the game. Sometimes a religious symbol circled their necks, or a lucky coin lay buried in their pocket or a red ribbon was pinned somewhere on their clothing to ward off evil spirits. Included in this mishmash of superstitious rituals they adhered to was the importance of sitting in the same chair every Friday. Several times, I had curiously watched as each man claimed his unspoken territory unchallenged.

When Sam arrived earlier than the rest that night, he plopped himself down on a chair normally sat in by Abe, one of the regulars. When Abe came into the cottage, he said congenially, "Hey Sam, I usually sit in the place you're in. Would you mind switching?"

"Well," Sam said, as he lit his cigarette, "sure looks like I'm sitting in it now and I'm sorta settled in." Easy going Abe simply chose another spot but as the rest of the guys came in, they were not as easily mollified. Charley grumbled about having lost his spot near the window. Joe griped that he was now downwind of all the cigarette smoke. Freddie complained he was doomed to be the biggest loser because Lady Luck wouldn't know where to find him. Earl groused about guests taking over. Dad quietly took the last chair remaining.

He slashed open two new packs of Bicycle playing cards, then pulled the heavy wrought iron chandelier closer to the table for more light. "Let the games begin," he announced cheerfully, and my sisters and I left the parlor to play Monopoly out on the veranda.

From outside we could hear Sam loudly crowing after each pot he won. "And that's the way it's done folks," he'd chuckled as he raked in his winnings.

As each man took his turn dealing, the dealer called out the cards, giving a running commentary on the developing hands, "Looks like somebody's flushing. Straight comin' up. Deuces never loses!" The fellas enjoyed the accompanying banter as it was a fun way to liven up their game. After only a couple of rounds, Sam exploded, "Hey! Just play poker. Forget the damn gabbing. We have eyes. We can all see what's goin' on."

Immediately, a frosty atmosphere emerged. There was no kidding around, no good-natured chitchat. "Come on already," Sam bullied the slower players, "For crying out loud, make a move in this lifetime," he growled. "Stay in or get out of the way."

Al was Sam's favorite target that night because of his slow, methodical moves. Sam mocked him by feigning such loud snoring sounds; we could clearly hear him from the porch. He harangued Earl constantly about keeping his cards on the table instead of laying them on his lap. When it was finally time for them to pause for their evening break, there was a communal sigh.

Unfortunately for Sam, when play was resumed, Lady Luck had taken her leave of him. Frantic, he stayed in, time after time, raising bets with an aplomb the cards did not warrant. Soon his winnings had disappeared, and he was now betting with his own money. His rage at this turn of events escalated with each tough loss he bore.

After Freddie won an extremely large pot, one Sam had bet on heavily, he slammed his mediocre cards onto the table with fury. "Hey Sam, take it down a notch," Dad warned.

Earl won the next two hands in a row. "Keep your damn cards on the table, not on your lap," Sam roared each time Earl collected his winnings.

"You're a guest at this game, so why don't you shut your big mouth?" Earl said.

A new hand was dealt. Sam glanced at his cards, smiled and raised the original wager. When it was Earl's turn, he met and raised Sam's bet. The other players had stayed in for a while but eventually all turned over their cards to indicate they were out of the competition. Only Earl and Sam remained, vying for what was now, a very large win.

Furious that Earl had not conceded as he surely expected him too, Sam snarled. "Ya got a few hidden goodies on your lap to pull out when you need them? Sure has to be a reason you're winning like crazy all of a sudden," he scoffed.

From our vantage point, we saw Earl had pulled himself up to a standing position. He was over six feet tall and physically imposing. "Are you calling me a cheater, Sam? You're losing because you're an ignoramus."

Instantly, Sam also got up and stood as tall as a five-foot three-inch guy can. He raised his right fist and let fly in an attempt to punch out his nemesis. Earl nimbly stepped out of his path and Sam's fist collided with the thorny, wrought iron chandelier that had been lowered earlier. The unwieldy fixture swung wildly about before finally smashing into Abe's face. Blood gushed from his nose, down his face and onto the table, soaking cards, coins and dollars lying there. An ashtray overflowing with cigarette butts crashed to the floor and scattered.

Everyone—the women playing pinochle, guests in the cottage, my sisters and me—rushed into the parlor to see what the commotion was about. We milled around the table in shock, stunned that a friendly game of cards had so quickly turned into a melee. Milly stood alone near the rear of the room, eyes wide, one hand covering her mouth.

"This poker game is over," Dad announced. "Al, split the money seven ways and give everyone his share."

"Hey, Harry. You just wait a minute!" Sam bellowed. "Not everyone was part of that last hand! I had a lotta money riding on that pot. It's not fair," he moaned. Dad cast a steely look at him. "We've all heard enough of what you have to say tonight. Split it seven ways, Al."

Even though Mother had patched together an ice pack for Abe, it had not stanched the flow of blood from his wounded nose. He and his wife soon left in search of medical care, even as Sam continued his rant. "Earl's been baiting me all night. This has nothin' to do with me that Abe got hurt. The doofus went and got himself in the middle. You all saw it. It's not my fault."

In a blessed silence, the pot was divided into seven portions. As each man exited the cottage, no one glanced Sam's way or replied to anything he had to say.

Milly collected her husband and steered him to the doorway, murmuring apologies to my parents. Sam screamed at her. "What in hell are you sorry for? Most of the money in that last pot was mine and they stole it." Sam slammed the screen door as he stalked out and Milly meekly followed behind him.

By the following Friday night, all the regular poker players were reunited, even the convalescing Jake. By then, Dad had installed a brand-new lighting fixture, securely attached to a stud in the ceiling, and the offending wrought iron menace had been tossed into the trash.

Dad looked out at the men seated near him, eager to play, yet gentlemen all.

Happily, he announced, "Let the games begin!"

17
The Quilt

Unused to the solitude of our winter household after a frenzied Majestic summer, Mother decided to try quilting to pass the time. Even though she had absolutely no idea how to proceed, that reality didn't faze her even slightly. She purchased a brand new, store-made quilt, and using a seam ripper, took it completely apart to see how it had been constructed.

The first time my sister and I accompanied Mother to the fabric shop, her list of supplies was long. She spent a lot of time selecting different colored cotton fabrics and added batting and flannel for warmth. She also purchased a special cutting tool, many spools of threads, sewing needles, mats and a three-foot ruler for measuring. As we left the shop loaded with our bags, Mother exclaimed, "I can't wait to start putting together my first quilt."

Instantly, yet not willingly, my sister and I became involved in Mother's newest passion as did our dad. Myrna and I carefully basted the raw edges of printed cloth our father had cut into precise squares while mother ironed them flat. My family found ourselves clustered together around the dining room table every night after supper, listening to the radio as we snipped and sewed.

After laying out several pieces of the hemmed squares on a mat, Mother said, "Look how wonderful this looks. We are going to have so much fun putting this together."

Anyone who has ever constructed a quilt for the first time knows that what she was doing was just the first timid step into the unknown. Soon challenge after challenge appeared, requiring more skill than she had, causing Mother to falter. "I had no idea how time-consuming making one of these things was," she said, rubbing her tired eyes after a long day of stitching square after square together.

By the end of the week, when it came time for her to add batting and flannel to the backing of the quilt, we began to sense her irritability after countless attempts to get everything aligned before stitching. In the dining room where her sewing machine and ironing board now lived, poufs of batting floated in the air; mosaics composed of cloth scraps covered the rugs and loose threads clung to everything. "Oh my God," Mother exclaimed, "What did I get myself into?"

Dad kept encouraging her, "Honey, you're almost there. You're getting really close to the finish line. Don't give up now."

"Wow," Mother said when the quilt was finally declared done, "I feel as though I've created a possible heirloom." The next day we returned to the fabric shop for more supplies and that evening, we plunged into creating a second heirloom.

Mother said she hoped to complete three quilts, now that she was more experienced in the art of quilting, before the cottage opened in spring. Unfortunately, the second one was not completely finished by then, even with all our help. One of my mother's greatest faults was underestimating the time involved in a project when she was in the throes of creativity. To me, quilt making was a grueling, time-consuming endeavor, but she differed. "I have made something strong and beautiful that will last for years."

By April, she was itching to get back to the Majestic, so eager was she to see how the one finished quilt would look on our old-fashioned metal beds. Our cottage had four identical upstairs rooms differentiated by color only: blue, pink, green and yellow. All were similarly decorated with a full-sized bed, a reading lamp, a dresser and summer spreads in colors matching their walls. Mother decided the quilt she had just finished should go in the yellow upstairs bedroom to make up for the inconvenience of the lack of an upstairs bathroom. Second floor occupants had to walk down several steps, then span almost the entire length of the cottage to get to a bathroom.

Once Mother laid the quilt across the bed, I had to admit it added warmth and a kind of old-world charm to the utilitarian bedroom. It was an instant upgrade.

On the first Monday the cottage opened, Mrs. Kurtz from the blue room came downstairs in a snit. "Mrs. Zarne, how come I didn't get a quilt for my room too? You know I've been coming here a lot longer than the Horowitz couple in the yellow room."

"Where it ended up was by chance," Mother explained, "but the good news is that I am almost finished with a second one, and as soon as it's done, you can have it. You're in the blue room, right?" Mrs. Kurtz smiled.

A few days later when Mother gave her the coveted quilt, Mrs. Kurtz couldn't resist showing it off to Belle, occupant of the pink room and Delores, occupant of the green room, now the only upstairs tenants without new bed coverings.

Belle and Delores requested a few words with Mother about the inequality of quilt distribution in the pastel-tinted bedrooms of the Majestic. The problem now was there were none left. Mother bought two new quilts of different designs in Buffalo and brought them back to the cottage. While the women were somewhat satisfied, they strongly protested that they didn't feel these new quilts met the higher standard set forth in what had been crafted for the yellow and blue rooms.

It wasn't too long before some of the renters on the first floor of the Majestic felt left out and passed over regarding the special treatment the upstairs folks had received. Resentment brewed. Finally Mother penned one of her signs announcing the strict criteria for the distribution of her quilts: "Only the bedrooms furthest away from toilets were eligible."

More tenants returned and learned about the unique bed coverings

Mother had crafted, and I began hearing the expression "Golden Hands" when her name was mentioned. The quilts were brought downstairs by the favored occupants to be viewed and admired. Many of our tenants pleaded with her to sew them one for their homes, but she was firm in her decision never to sell them. "My handiwork is a labor of love," she declared. "They will never be displayed anywhere except on the beds of the Majestic." The truth was that these quilts were so much work, no one could ever pay her enough to make them one.

One of our most outspoken tenants said jokingly, "What if I just take one when I go home and leave you a twenty-dollar bill? What could you possibly do?" Mother playfully answered, "I'd call the Canadian Mounties to rescue my quilts." Even though everyone laughed, I wondered if there was a real possibility of someone just walking off with one like that.

Mother and Dad were naïve in business matters and hadn't protected themselves against theft or damaged property in any way since their losses had always been irrelevant: a shattered tea cup or a lost kitchen towel, but now the quilts were the most valuable items in the cottage.

The plan they devised to thwart possible quilt-loving robbers was to gather the quilts up the day before a tenant's departure and replace it with a blanket. This was accomplished on the pretense that the quilts required laundering between occupancies.

Many times Mother said she wished she had taken up embroidery or knitting to pass away the winter hours even if they didn't present as much of a challenge as quilting did.

Ultimately, she buckled under pressure and agreed to sew two more quilts by the following summer for the pink and green rooms. Our own personal living space was never graced with one of them. When the last two were completed for the cottage, Mother joyfully tossed out all her scraps of material and special tools.

She was correct in knowing that her hand-sewn quilts would stand the test of time. When the cottage was sold many years later, they were left on the beds still in remarkably good condition. The new owners of the Majestic fawned over them just as many others had in past years.

Golden Hands had made them.

18
The Luckiest Boy

Sure, I had heard about the opulent house owned by the Cotters in Sherkston Beach. It was in an exclusive neighborhood on the Canadian side of Lake Erie where upper class Canadians and Americans spent their summers. Although only a couple of miles from the Majestic, here were many large homes that overlooked private beaches on Lake Erie. Their owners hired gardeners from the village to tend to the grounds and housekeepers to take care of the interior and do some cooking. Most of these residents belonged to country clubs in nearby towns.

This was the same beach and Canadian coastline we all shared yet the landscape here bore the pristine appearance money creates. There was an artistry in the dunes' wild formations on the beach amidst professionally tamed shrubbery on the lawns. The homes were set far apart from one another on grassy inclines, and from the outside they seemed uninhabited. However, as one rounded the curved road, a backward glance revealed people cavorting on the beach, sunning on decks, swimming in the water, completely cut off from the masses we dealt with on our part of the lake.

Our adventure took place at the end of one August when summer's final days approached, and everything was winding down. Many tourists had already abandoned the beaches for their winter homes. Much of what my friends and I had enjoyed had grown stale and we were eager for something exciting to do. We wanted a challenge, a quest, an adventure, and when Robin and her brother, Jay, first came up with a unique idea, we were enthralled—frightened yet in total agreement.

The following morning, five of us, young teens at the time, met to go on a long bike ride and picnic. Each of us had packed lunches, filled thermos bottles and doffed caps against the heat of the sun to come. We rode single file on country roads behind Jay who had assumed leadership of our makeshift group's journey to a special destination.

After several miles, we arrived at a large summer home overlooking the shoreline that was announced by a simple sign that said, "The Cotters," no cutesy nickname like others in that neighborhood.

We knew that Wanda, a year-round Crystal Beach resident, came out to the Cotter's weekly to clean and replenish supplies. Her husband Henry tended the grounds. People passing by sometimes spotted Wanda watering the large urns of geraniums or sweeping up the veranda or Henry weeding flower beds or mowing the lawn. The Cotters, however, had never been seen anywhere, not on the porch, on the beach or even in the village. If no one lived there, why were Wanda's services required weekly? It didn't make sense.

The day we decided to do some sleuthing was one when we knew Wanda and Henry would not be around. We parked our bikes in a shady area nearby and while we lunched, we observed the house, watching patiently to see if anyone came around.

Jay and his sister decided they would rap on the front door and should someone answer, simply ask for directions to somewhere else. The brother and sister were fearless. I hung back with my other friends, half hidden by the bushes. I observed safely from across the street waiting to see what would happen.

Jay knocked on the door several times but there was no response. Robin turned the knob and the door swung open. She and Jay slipped inside, shouting greetings to whoever might possibly be there. Brazenly they advanced more deeply inside the beach house. A smiling Robin returned to the doorway after a few minutes to beckon us in. I found myself crossing the street, walking up the steps, crossing the threshold into the Cotter's house as if hypnotized.

The oversized, well-furnished area I walked into had louvered windows that faced the lake. I cranked open one of the windows to alleviate the stuffiness of the room. Gossamer, white-paneled sheers that adorned those windows billowed inwards and brilliant light flooded the room. I stepped out onto the wooden deck, furnished with overstuffed chaise loungers, umbrella tables, pots of flowers. Seeing the beach from this lofty view, made me feel as if I had never seen this landscape before now. It lay before me in its natural state, primal and untouched. The solitude intensified every sound: the waves as they smashed to shore, the birds as they cawed overhead. I breathed in the honeyed air wafting off the lake. This unique view was what the Cotters awoke to each morning. My ability to experience it, too, was definitely worth the chance I was taking by being here uninvited.

The living room was furnished with white wicker furniture upholstered in a small navy print and adorned with plump pillows. Floor to ceiling shelves were filled with books, and I noticed many framed photographs of a boy being hugged by a couple I assumed were his parents. There were smiling pictures from the boy's infancy to the present where he appeared to be about six or seven years old. My glance fell to the far side of the bookcase and there was a snapshot that had been left face down, unframed.

The child had been photographed standing alone on this isolated beach, his home in the background. The sky looked dark and dismal, and I guessed the picture had been taken in early spring as there were patches of snow amidst sparse greenery. The boy wore a heavy looking pea coat, a plaid scarf wrapped around his neck and he grasped a cap in his hand. His hair was flung about by the wind. Despite the bulkiness of his clothing, he looked thin, his face gaunt and pale. I quickly replaced the photo where I found it, face down.

Emboldened by the emptiness of the beach house, we ventured into the bedrooms. Robin and I swung open drawers and rummaged in closets. We flung Mrs. Cotter's beautiful scarves and beaded shawls over our shoulders, adorned ourselves with her many necklaces, earrings, and bangles. Robin and I anointed our bodies with her scented lotions and lavishly sprayed perfumes that smelled of spring flowers on ourselves. As we had when we were little girls, we were playing dress-up again but with props far more elegant. It was exhilarating to parade about in all this finery, pretending we were something we were not.

The boy's bedroom was just the kind we imagined a privileged child would have. Painted white shelving overflowed with toys, board games, and books. He had his own television and a private adjoining bath. Large quantities of clothing overwhelmed his closets. Here indeed, lived a lucky boy, someone who had so much more than his allotted share.

My friends were in the kitchen busily removing items from the fridge and eating whatever looked appetizing to them. Out came gourmet cheeses, cokes, a jar of pickles, a bowl of cherries. In the well-stocked cupboards, we found expensive chocolates, crackers, cookies, fancy canned nuts. We tossed everything on their granite, kitchen table. We drank colas from the Cotters' fancy glasses and ate off their fine plates, feeling justified and deserving of this largess. It was obscene that some people had so very much money, I thought with envy.

Robin went snooping through their kitchen desk. "There's a folder here with Wanda's name on it," she shrieked. Quickly everyone joined her as she poked and prodded. Inside the folder she found a contract signed by Wanda and her husband, unconditionally agreeing to maintain confidentiality about the Cotter family. No surprise there. We also found strange instructions for Wanda to keep everything at the house in a constant state of readiness, should their family wish to come out unexpectedly. This was Joey's favorite place in the world, Mrs. Cotter had written. Ha, I chuckled, the rich and their entitled ways.

We rummaged through more receipts, which were mostly for food and gardening supplies. As we probed further, we found another file with a stack of medical invoices that had been paid in late May. Among them were prescription charges and paid bills indicating treatment for ailments described in five-syllable medical terms we had never heard of. These were all for the care of the young Joey Cotter, age seven. Their lucky boy was very ill, and it seemed to have something to do with his blood. Even though we didn't know what he was sick from, it looked like what Joey had was extremely serious.

Wordlessly, we returned the file to where we found it. In the master bedroom, my friends and I carefully refolded Mrs. Cotter's' lovely things and reunited her jewelry with their velvet boxes. We re-capped the perfume dispensers, tightened lotion bottles and swept way spilt powders. Joey's books and games were realigned the way they had been before we came in uninvited.

Robin and I wiped down the kitchen table, swept the floor, and closed the louvered windows. Empty soda bottles, half consumed bags of chips, chocolate wraps and cherry pits went into a garbage bag the boys took with us when we exited. All was left neat, and hopefully, everything would appear untouched. We trekked out of the cottage, our heads low, and shut the front door behind us. Single file, we bicycled down the country roads behind Jay back to our own, less affluent side of the lake. Silently we parted and the events of that afternoon were never brought up or discussed again.

During the long winter months in Buffalo, I often thought about that little boy named Joey. I hoped he was alright and maybe even thriving. I could never relive that trespassing incident without feeling intense pangs of remorse.

It was only a few days after our return to the Majestic the following summer, that I found myself bicycling down those long, winding roads to the Cotter's beach house alone. Their place bore the familiar, forsaken, appearance it had last summer yet something was changed. The wood sign proclaiming this as Cotter's property had been thrown on the lawn. Hammered into the grass instead was another sign announcing this property sold.

I suddenly became aware that even though I didn't know them personally, I knew a lot more about the Cotters than I ever should have known, and I knew with certainty why they no longer needed their beach house. Blinking back tears, I slowly pedaled away.

19
The Throwaway

There was an undeniably classic look about Mrs. Koster. She was an attractive, slender woman whose glossy black hair had been pulled taut into a chignon. Her makeup was subtly applied, and diamond studs nestled in her ear lobes. On that hot June day, she was dressed in a navy blue suit and high heeled pumps, attire far more suitable for an air-conditioned office than the Lake Erie Canadian beach.

Her husband sat quietly slouched in a chair thumbing through a newspaper while his wife did the talking. She was arrogant, spoke in an authoritative manner, and pointed a manicured finger at whomever she was addressing. She was employed as a private assistant to a corporate executive in Toronto. Her job required a lot of traveling, and that is what brought her here this summer to the Majestic.

"I think my daughter should be occupied rather than left alone in the city, so I thought why not rent her a room here for the season just like any other boarder?" Mrs. Koster questioned with an unmistakable air of haughtiness. "I'm willing to pay double your weekly rate just so Marnie's included in family meals and is allowed to do her laundry here. She's a capable girl and will be no bother."

Marnie, who had just turned fifteen a few weeks ago, stood silently by as her mother planned her forthcoming summer. Mrs. Koster kept reassuring Mother that Marnie was a mild, submissive girl, and indeed Marnie appeared to be so. She offered no protest nor comment regarding this unconventional arrangement. The Majestic rooms had always been rented out to families, never to unaccompanied adolescents.

Dad voiced his concern, but the fact that Marnie's mother was going to pay so generously for her board dispelled most of my parents' uneasiness. It was agreed her daughter would stay with us. Mrs. Koster slapped crisp hundred-dollar bills into my mother's hands and briskly counted them off as she did. "I'm leaving cash for Marnie's personal expenses to be given her weekly," she said as she thrust twelve envelopes at my mother. "We'll see you again on the first Sunday of September." From across the room she addressed her daughter solemnly: "You do as you're told." She picked up her bag and quickly exited the cottage followed by her husband. Their black sedan rolled away from the curb toward Toronto and Marnie was left behind with us.

She stood forlornly in a corner of the parlor amidst suitcases and duffle bags, twisting her hands nervously and shifting her body aimlessly from side to side. Dad came forward to welcome this piteous girl. "Hi Marnie," he smiled. "Let me help you get all those bags up to your room." Addressing me, he asked that some cold drinks be set up on the porch so we could all get acquainted.

I studied Marnie with disdain as we sat there on the porch. She was a plain, dark-eyed girl with an elongated face and straight black hair, cut in a Prince Valiant hairstyle. She was outfitted in clothing more suitable for someone much younger than fifteen, maybe purposely, but no one could ignore the fact that this young girl, while hardly pretty, was extremely shapely.

My parents chose me to entertain Marnie and show her around the area. The first few weeks were a lot of fun. Money for her personal expenses had been provided and was dispersed to Marnie weekly as instructed. These envelopes contained fifty dollars in cash for Marnie to spend however she wished. This was an enormous amount of money at a time when that much cash could feed a family of five comfortably for a week.

I quickly learned Marnie could be easily manipulated as to how her allowance should be spent. "Hey Marnie, let's go for Chinese food. Hey Marnie, what about the new movie that just opened? How 'bout bowling?" My new best friend and I spent a lot of time shopping together with reckless abandon wherever we went. It was a heady experience for me not to have to consider the cost of anything.

"Thank you so much, Marnie," I'd exclaim after she paid for the cute sundresses and lacy sandals I had picked out for myself. The only requirement for this largess was to smile at her in gratitude and merchandise I could never have afforded was suddenly mine.

Marnie was two years older than me, yet I always felt the elder. She insisted that I make every decision, even over the simplest things such as what she should order when we went out to eat. She consistently sought my approval regarding her choices. I was beginning to grasp just how needy she was. It began to become a burden.

In the three weeks Marnie had been with us there was no communication from her parents as to her welfare. They had simply placed her with us, people she didn't know anything about, then had forgotten that their daughter existed. I felt sorry for this woeful girl, yet realized that I would never have sought her out to be my friend. With each day that passed, I found myself more and more disenchanted with Marnie. I had begun to feel very uncomfortable about how much money she spent on me and angry at myself for allowing it to continue unrestrained. I resented her more each day.

Ultimately, my anger was unleashed at my parents for saddling me with her simply because we were somewhat close in age. "You took her in for the summer and suddenly I'm her nursemaid," I screamed. "I have to pretend that she's my best buddy. You have absolutely no idea how boring she is, and everyone I introduce her to thinks she's a weirdo, and none of my friends want anything to do with her," I complained.

"Marnie's a guest at the Majestic and deserves to be treated well," Dad said, and that was the end of my tantrum.

I snuck out of the cottage whenever possible, ignoring Marnie's woebegone puppy dog look when I left alone or passed her by on the beach, pretending not to see her as I sought out more animated companionship. No longer would I include her in any activity.

In mid-July, a college fraternity rented a cottage a block away from where we lived. They painted a large wooden sign canary yellow and nailed it to their front tree. The exuberant tenants named the cottage "The Mardi Grad" and christened it with several half-empty bottles of beer. They partied late into the night, every night.

The frat boys took quick notice of Marnie as she sunned alone on the beach. She looked cute in the new two-piece bathing suit picked up on one of our recent shopping sprees. The guys flirted with her constantly and a transformed, fun-loving Marnie emerged from all this attention, and she immediately forgot all about me. Suddenly, my days were my own again.

Her generosity was deflected from me to her new frat friends. They would all go to the market, and she would stock their fridge and pantry to overflowing. Marnie bragged about how she'd slipped them money for beer and cigarettes and about all the many places she took them out to eat. Could she seriously have thought I'd be jealous?

Marnie was extremely popular at the Mardi Grad and within just a week or so stopped sleeping at the Majestic altogether, preferring the freewheeling atmosphere at the frat house where a party was always going on.

She stopped by our cottage merely to collect her allowance. She reeked of alcohol and cigarettes. This situation truly upset my father. Marnie was only fifteen years old and although the boys were barely young adults themselves, he felt that they were taking advantage of her naïveté.

"Hey Marnie! Have you got a minute?" my father said one day. "I want to talk to you about something that's been bothering me." He led her to a quiet spot in the backyard and they settled into some wicker chairs. "You're a very nice girl," he began, "but I'm concerned that those boys at the Mardi Grad are much too wild for you to be hanging around with." Dad stuttered at this point. "They're more mature and at a sexually different point in their lives than you."

His face reddened and his stutter grew worse, but he continued on. Marnie listened attentively, her eyes never leaving his, her chin in her hands and nodding her head in agreement as he spoke.

"Don't you worry about me, Mister Harry," she smiled as she blithely assured him, "I'm doing alright." She kissed the top of his head and then scurried back to the Mardi Grad.

"I'm going to call her family and tell them what's going on," Dad said with finality. "She's way too young to be left here alone unsupervised." Mother called what he intended to do "meddling." With much trepidation he grabbed our newly installed phone and dialed the Toronto number, hands shaking.

"Sorry to bother you folks," he began nervously, "but there's a fraternity cottage nearby packed with college boys and Marnie's been sleeping over there every night. Even though she's a sweet kid, we can't have her here anymore without a guardian. It was our mistake, and we'll give you a full refund, but you need to come and get your girl back home," he finished.

"You're only paid to be her landlord not her keeper," Mrs. Koster said, and in an even voice she reminded him that they had a verbal contract. "I have no intention whatsoever of reclaiming her before September. Don't concern yourself about my daughter's innocence," she scoffed. "I don't. I had that idiot child sterilized a year ago," she shouted and the phone went dead.

The raucous parties these boys had would start late afternoon and continue throughout the evening until dawn. Our cottage wasn't bothered by the constant racket that emanated from the Mardi Grad, but their behavior seriously infringed upon the quieter lifestyle of one of the closer neighbors, and he promptly called the Ontario Provincial Police.

Most everyone at the Majestic was awakened about three in the morning by two stern-looking officers banging loudly on our front door. It required the strength of both officers to keep a staggering, disheveled Marnie upright. She had been found drunk in bed with two young boys when the police arrived. The boys claimed ignorance when informed she was only fifteen, and Marnie claimed she had freely consented to be there.

The guys involved were neither arrested nor charged. Instead, they were ordered to vacate their cottage by ten o'clock the next morning, leave it clean and keep their mouths shut about the entire incident. Frightened and instantly sober, the frat brothers knew they were very lucky to have gotten off so easily. Because Crystal Beach was a family vacation spot, the authorities routinely hushed up incidents of this sort to maintain its wholesome image.

One of the officers called Marnie's parents. He ordered them in very harsh words to get their daughter back to Toronto immediately or face charges. My parents did not escape the anger of the police for allowing a minor to stay with them unsupervised. The police laid the blame squarely at their feet.

Marnie passed out on the sofa, the police left, and the folks in the Majestic tried to settle down and get back to sleep. Mother and I gathered up Marnie's belongings and packed them into the suitcases and duffle bags she had brought with her. Dad carried everything out to the front porch, and after that, we sat tense and nervous, just staring at the clock. Marnie slept nearby, unaware of all the angst she had caused and actions she had thrust into motion.

Marnie awoke just in time to get to the bathroom where her sobering up process involved being very sick. When the worst was over, she fell back on the sofa and Dad brought a cool cloth for her head. "I'm so sorry. I'm so sorry," she kept repeating to him as he patted her hand.

Her parents arrived at the cottage as the sun was coming up. Mrs. Koster's hair was a tangled mess, and without makeup, she was a very plain woman. Her husband looked exhausted. He silently gathered up Marnie's belongings from the porch, transferred them to his car trunk, and waited in the front seat for his family to join him. Mrs. Koster roughly shook her daughter. "C'mon. Get up. You've caused enough trouble for one night. It's time to go."

Even though dreadfully unsteady, Marnie shoved her mother's arm brusquely away when she attempted to help her. She finally managed to regain her balance and teeter over to where my parents and I waited to say our goodbyes. My father said to Marnie, "I'm sorry this ended like this. We wish you all the best."

Marnie pulled herself up straight and whispered, "Thank you for the best summer of my whole life. You were all so nice to me." She reached for my dad's hand and kissed his fingers, "Especially you."

Wordlessly, Mrs. Koster shoved her daughter away and exited the cottage. We saw a tearful Marnie waving goodbye to us from the rear window of the car as they drove away, and we continued to wave back at her until the car was completely out of view.

After Marnie was gone, her final words to us haunted me for days. I realized Marnie had been exceptionally gracious in her expression of gratitude when she included all three of us, but not all three of us were deserving of that gratitude. The only one among us who had shown her any kindness or humanity or exhibited any concern for her, had always been my father. I had not thought of Marnie as being especially perceptive, yet she was the one most keenly aware of his innate decency.

We never crossed paths with Marnie or her family again, yet I often wondered how her life turned out. My dad had wished her well. Hopefully she is.

20
First Stirrings

The screen door creaked open and there he was. Certainly the most beautiful boy/man I had ever seen. I must have stared, certainly, too dumbfounded to speak. "Hey, excuse me," he said, "I'm looking for the proprietor. I'm interested in renting here at the Majestic. Do you know who I should ask for?"

"Oh yes! Yes!" I stammered. "That would be my mother. Let me get her for you." I had muttered the words but hadn't moved off the swing I had been sitting on. The book I had been reading still lay on my lap. I just stared at him mesmerized.

"Should I come back later?" he asked confused. Those words catapulted me off the swing and jolted me into action.

"Oh no, wait. She's out back. I'll get her for you. You wait here. She'll be right out. Don't move." If I could have tied him in place, I would have.

Mother was in the back yard watering flowers. "There's a guy waiting on the porch to talk to you." I gasped. "I think he wants to rent a room. Hurry. Come quickly. He's absolutely gorgeous."

I tossed the watering can away from her hands and pulled her back into the cottage through to the front porch. He was still there leaning casually against the porch railing. When we came out, he smiled and introduced himself as Steve. I could see my mother was instantly charmed by him, too.

They sat around a white wicker table to talk, and I made sure I was near enough to hear their conversation. He was a Buffalo college student and had just finished his freshman year. Steve had secured a job at the amusement park for the summer. He had decided it might be a good idea to live at Crystal Beach for the season and forego spending the summer in New York City where he was from.

Steve was close to six feet tall, with attractive features, wavy brown hair, chocolate-colored eyes and a sturdy physique. I was absolutely smitten by this fellow that I hadn't even known existed thirty minutes ago.

It was the last day of June, and one of our two cabins was available for a season's rental. Steve planned on sharing the cabin's cost with a college buddy, Rick, who also had a job at the park. Mother and Steve settled on a weekly rate and arrangements were made to have the cabin ready for them the following day so they could move in over the weekend.

He and Rick barely had time to get settled before they started working in the park.

They were ushers at the Crystal Ballroom, a job I thought was glamorous. They had to dress in regimental clothing supplied by the management. Their uniforms were beige and adorned with thin strips of gold braiding on the jacket cuffs, the lapel, and down the outer seam of the trousers. The Crystal Ballroom ushers wore stiff brimmed military hats decorated with the same thin gold braiding.

The ushers were the ones that maintained order in the dance-hall. The Crystal Ballroom was open to all spectators for free but if someone chose to dance, a special ticket had to be purchased. Each dance lasted about fifteen minutes, and then the ushers like Steve and Rick would grab an end of a long, crimson velvet rope, stretch it across the dance floor and walk forward in unison, rope in hand. The dance area would become smaller and smaller, forcing the participants gently off the floor to make way for the next group of ticket holders already in line.

Every night I would cajole one of my friends or my sister Myrna to come to the dancehall simply to watch Steve in his manly uniform bring order to the Crystal Ballroom. "I don't want to keep coming here night after night," Myrna complained. "We're too young to dance even if someone should ask us, which, by the way, has never happened and probably never will!"

Myrna was right. There were so many older pretty girls there and no one ever noticed us behind the rails. Many of those cute girls flirted with Steve and Rick, though. Besides being good looking guys, they looked important and authoritative in their uniforms. They were consistently pleasant and polite to the girls, but kept their distance. It probably was one of the rules of management, I guessed, not to mingle while working, and if it was, that was one rule I thoroughly applauded.

After the park closed, usually after midnight, the guys would come back to the cottage, change into shorts and tee shirts, guzzle cokes, munch on chips and sit out in back of the cottage kibitzing with Myrna and me late into the night. Steve was so easy to listen to. Sometimes he would show off his knowledge about a brilliant fact he had recently learned in class. He was very interested in science and would probably declare that as his major. Rick mostly listened like my sister and I did, but neither of them were as bedazzled as I was. Steve could have been reading a grocery list out loud and I would have been just as enthralled.

Mother really liked those boys. She didn't get a chance to cook too many fine meals at the cottage because she was always so busy, but she did prepare a nice dinner every Friday night. Steve and Rick didn't start their ballroom gig until the sun started to go down, so she often invited them to eat with us on Friday nights. Since neither of my parents had gone to college or had ever visited New York City, they were enraptured by the stories of campus life and what it was like growing up in such a big city. Steve had the gift of transforming the most mundane happening into an epic tale. How entertaining he was, and so courteous. And he and Rick insisted on doing the cleanup after dinner in appreciation of Mother's hospitality despite her efforts to dissuade them.

From the first moment I had laid eyes on Steve, I knew I loved him unequivocally, even though he seemed unattainable to me at this time in our lives. He was nineteen and I was thirteen. He was on the cusp of manhood, and I had just entered my teens.

Facts do not have a place in the heart, especially for a first love. I'd go to bed dreaming about him and hoping that in a few years Steve would look at me differently, with eyes of love and say something goofy like, "Where have you been all my life?" I would answer with words of enlightenment, "Right here, before your eyes," and we would gently kiss. In reality, Steve never acted any other way than as a kindly brother, but I had my own hopes and dreams about a future with him someday.

Summer was swiftly approaching its inevitable finale. Our winter home was only a fifteen-minute bus drive from Steve's university, so I didn't feel as sad as I might have had he been returning to New York to finish school there. Thankfully, Steve would continue to be a part of my life as my Mother extended an open invitation to Steve and Rick for Friday night dinners once we all moved back to the city.

One late evening as I was sitting on the porch swing, I heard a few of our tenants who were staying at the cottage talking about Steve and Rick. One woman said the guys had their arms around each other at the park when they thought no one they knew was about. Her husband said that he had also seen them hugging and kissing in the shelter of the grove. My first reaction was "so what;" the guys were really close. The conversation took on a more sinister tone when another tenant mentioned strange sounds emanating from the cabin the guys shared as he walked through the backyard to his own cabin just the other night.

"Stop lying," I screamed, moving out of the shadows so they could see me. "You don't know what you're talking about. They're close like brothers. God will punish you all for saying such terrible things." Actually, I didn't really know exactly what they were referring to, but the implications sounded ominous to me. How dare they say these things about the young man I fervently hoped would be much more than a friend someday.

Mom and Dad were already in bed when I burst in, hysterically crying as I tried to explain what I had just heard about Steve and Rick. I was barely able to talk through my tears and hiccups and cries of disbelief. My parents exchanged one of their looks. Dad got out of bed and brought me a glass of water while I continued my frenzied ranting, desperately waiting for them to make everything okay again.

I choked on the water as I listened in horror while Dad stumbled through an explanation of love between two men. My mother said, "This shouldn't make any difference in how you feel about them. They're good boys."

"My God. You both knew," I gasped, "and no one ever mentioned anything to me about it".

Dad sighed, "We really couldn't see how this would affect you, so why would we bring it up?" I was speechless.

Mother said, "I knew the first time Steve brought Rick over to meet us. I could see the way they looked at each other."

"Oh my God. Oh my God," I wailed, "It can't be, I love Steve! I love him!"

My parents looked at each other sadly, finally understanding my intense reaction to this revelation. I had kept my emotions so well hidden they had not realized that I had romantic feelings for Steve. He was the first guy I really cared for.

After that earthshaking discovery, things were never the same. It hurt way too much. It was our age difference that I had believed to be the real obstacle between us, an obstacle that would be overcome by time. I was embarrassed by my naiveté. While I worshipped Steve, Steve worshipped Rick.

When the relationship between Steve and Rick became common knowledge at the cottage, my mother refused to say anything negative about the situation. "It's hard enough to find someone you love in this life, so what's the big deal," she asked those who were shocked or indignant or judgmental. It wasn't the reaction they expected. I think they expected her to immediately throw them out in a furor of condemnation.

The last few weeks they were at the Majestic they kept strictly to themselves. I knew it was because of me. I neither acknowledged nor spoke to either of them. There was absolutely no way for me to grant myself permission to accept Steve for being who he was. Unlike the kindness shown to them by my parents, I behaved badly and simply didn't care.

My family was very cordial to the guys when it was time to say goodbye. Mother kissed their cheeks, Dad shook their hands and wished them good luck in their studies, and Myrna and Linda gave them big hugs.

I stood silently by and barely glanced at them while this leave-taking was going on. I'm sure Steve thought it was because I disapproved of his relationship with Rick but that was not the case. Even if my feelings were irrational, I was furious and devastated that Steve was so incapable of loving me as I did him. He had broken my heart even if he was unaware of it.

When they were finally gone, I wept because we had once been good friends. Then I wept even more wretchedly because that's all we could ever be to one another.

21
Time Of Reckoning

The sun had begun its slow descent, and the park was beginning to come alive as evening approached. For Mother, my sisters, and me, it was as if time had completely stopped. We were all clustered together on a hard wooden bench near where the *S.S. Canadiana* daily ferried passengers to Crystal Beach from Buffalo.

None of us spoke. I could see my mother's hands trembling as she clutched them tightly together, a thin film of perspiration glazed her forehead. She sat there unmoving, jaw clenched, her frightened eyes simply staring out at nothing, unaware of her surroundings or even of her frightened children beside her.

During the summer when we lived in the Majestic, Dad would wend his way from work to Buffalo's harbor every weekend and board the *S.S. Canadiana* to Crystal Beach. Every Friday night mother would cook a special dinner for him in anticipation of his two-day mini-holiday from work. On this night, however, the roasted chicken and root vegetables she had prepared had been left untouched, cold and congealing in the pan on top of the oven. As soon as we told her what had happened, she flung off her apron and raced through the park to the landing pier, my sisters and I trailing behind her in a zigzagged, frenzied chase.

Once we arrived at the pier, it was quite deserted as the last passengers had disembarked well over an hour ago. Ordinarily, both Myrna and I went together to welcome our dad when he came into port about six o'clock in the evening, but that night, Myrna had gone alone. She had seen Dad on the pier and indeed had waved to him and he to her, but Dad had not come through the gate that led into Canada. She waited, watching all the passengers disperse but Dad had not reappeared.

The enormous clock in the dance hall tower informed her she had been there for over three quarters of an hour waiting, but it had seemed much longer. She was twelve years old, alone and she must have been terrified. Myrna left the park in terror and ran quickly back to the cottage. The family had to be told that Daddy had disappeared, had not come off the *Canadiana* pier, had simply vanished. My sister reached the cottage bent over, gasping and so out of breath she was unable to speak. Mother's voice rose, "Dinner is going to be ruined! Where have you and your father been? I've been trying to keep things warm for almost an hour."

So, there we sat at the pier, unmoving, captured in this tableau of horrific fear. The entire area was dark except for a dimly lit immigration building set fifty feet away. Everyone who departed the *Canadiana* had to pass through that building toward the immigration officers' booths that guarded the turnstiles to be routinely questioned. There was no other way to get into Canada except through the iron metal gate that was locked after the last arrivals had come through. There was no one around but us, nor had we seen anyone come out of that building on the pier. We continued to sit there, wide-eyed and helpless.

Could Dad have gotten sick? Would he be unable to communicate because he was unconscious? Had he died suddenly? It was inconceivable that he would have gone anywhere willingly when he knew his daughters were anxiously waiting for him at the dock. Dear God, where was he? How long should we wait before we sought out the police?

The wrought iron lampposts on the pier cast scant light yet caught the eerie shadows and movements of the nearby trees around us. The terrified silence was interrupted only by the waves crashing against the break wall. This lively juncture was now one of desolation for us who kept watch. Even though time had plodded along, it still came as a shock to see the brightly lit *Canadiana* begin her over wide turn that preceded her second approach to Crystal Beach. She had completed the round-trip sail from here to Buffalo and then back to Crystal Beach again.

The *S.S. Canadiana* was a grand old Victorian queen of a ship. That night she sparkled and glowed with strings of twinkling lights that lit up the waves about her. Dance music drifted over the water as she headed toward shore. With certainty, we knew that people were twirling and spinning to the band's music, enjoying their wine or beer—so happy that the weekend had arrived. I couldn't imagine how the world could remain so ordinary, so commonplace when we despaired of ever seeing our father again. We all knew there was no way he would have forsaken us if everything was alright. Something had to be very wrong.

Morosely we watched the *Canadiana* steal ever closer to land. We remained paralyzed, immobile, and physically unable to leave this spot. Someone, somewhere, we dreaded, would eventually deliver what was sure to be bad news to us.

In the dim light Myrna suddenly spied two male figures slowly walking up the isolated pier. They had exited that small building so very far away and were now approaching us. We saw a uniformed guard coming toward us along with our father walking on his own, seemingly well.

The guard unlocked the gate and pulled it open. Dad stepped through and folded himself into our arms, his body trembling. He looked disheveled, his face white. Laughing and crying simultaneously, we assailed him with questions. *What happened? Are you hurt? Why were you there so long?* He held us all in a painfully tight embrace.

His voice was hoarse, he sounded so tired. "Not now! Let's just go home. I just want to get back home," he whispered.

We entered the midway of the park ablaze with color, lights, sounds of shouting and laughter. The roar of the roller coaster, the thumping and clattering of the amusement rides, the maniacal laughter emanating from the Fun House all seemed surreal and distorted to me. Through the park we strode, five abreast clutching one another, so thankful to be reunited once again. The calliope played gaily on as we trekked past the carousel toward the exit. Silently we continued to our refuge, the Majestic.

Even though it was after eleven o'clock when we got back, several of the guests peppered us with questions, seeking an explanation, as if they felt deserving of one too. Everyone there had been worried about Dad and concerned for us as we were gone so long. Dad waved them away wearily. "No. Not now. Not now. There was a misunderstanding. I'm fine. It was nothing," he mumbled as he passed quickly through the dining room, Mother at his side, to the safety of their bedroom.

Our nice dinner was ruined and inedible. The fresh bread we had bought earlier lay hardened and stale in its basket. Unused dinner plates remained on the table along with cutlery we had placed over folded napkins. The lemon Mother had sliced to be served with tea lay shriveled and dry. Myrna and I threw out the food, washed the dishes, switched on the night light, and then went to bed. We were happy to see the end of this day.

My sisters and I all fell asleep quickly and slept soundly through the night. The endless hours of tension and anxiety were past. Everything was all right in our world once again.

Our dad had come through Ellis Island with three younger siblings when he was a boy of seven, early in the twentieth century. Now a man in his forties, he simply never thought of himself as an immigrant after having lived in the United States most of his life. He was automatically a citizen under his father's passport. So sure was

Dad that no one would ever mistake him for an immigrant that he had gone over the border countless times confidently stating "USA" when asked where he was born.

Last night when he came through customs, as he had so many times before, an immigration agent detected something off in his speech. He was pulled from the line and interrogated. Dad reluctantly admitted he was born in Russia, explaining that he was an American citizen via his father's passport. He endured countless hours of questioning and when the authorities were finally convinced he was who he said he was, they allowed him entry into Canada. His father's ancient documents were valid, but Dad was told he had to apply for his own papers now as an adult. He was warned to take care of this as soon as possible.

Sheepishly, Dad admitted that the worst parts of this ordeal had been the unmasking of him as not being native born. He had so thoroughly loved the idea of being a true-blue patriotic American that he had almost forgotten he wasn't. Our father had trusted that his long lost, unused Slavic language of early childhood had been obliterated by his many years of living in the United States. "I've lived here so long, yet I am still considered an immigrant," he said sadly.

"But also an American," Mother reminded him.

He never again crossed the border without his passport. He'd pull it out of his jacket pocket with aplomb when asked to produce it. The official document was indisputable, undeniable proof of his right to be here, a privilege not to be taken lightly.

22
The Prize

The Majestic was only opened for occupancy until the last Sunday of August and only until noon. Right after lunch, my family gathered excitedly around the kitchen table; there was still something very important left for us to do. My mother brought out her old wooden cigar box from its hiding place, along with her black and white marbled notebook.

We took out all the cash and receipts for this past summer's rentals to see how our family had made out that year. The money had been squirreled away, untouched even for expenses, until this grand moment of revelation. The colorful Canadian bills were stacked into neat piles, counted and recounted, then carefully recorded in Mother's journal to see if they reconciled. We all looked forward to this exciting moment. How successful a summer had it been? The end of the Majestic season was akin to bringing in the harvest.

What Mother earned during the summer was considered our family's extra spending money. Everyone got some new clothes. Something special was purchased for our winter home in the States—an appliance, a piece of furniture, or maybe new carpeting. Never would it have occurred to my parents to celebrate a successful season with an extravagant dinner at an upscale restaurant. Rewards had to be something one could touch, look at and say, "Yup! I earned that." It had to be tangible.

Mother's personal present to herself was always something special from the Blakely's China Shoppe at season's end.

This boutique was located in the village of Ridgeway, two miles away from the beach. The store seemed out of place in such a small hamlet, but it was prosperous. It not only served summer tourists but also catered to affluent Americans interested in buying luxurious English imports for themselves or for gifts. Ridgeway was closer for Buffalonians to travel to than Toronto, Ontario, an additional hundred miles away. This was another of the many advantages of living so close to an international border.

Even though I had never seen a proper British china store, I imagined this is what they must all look like. Dark wood framed the store's windows that were separated into small panes of glass with wire dividers, making it look old and weathered. Although potential customers had to squint to see the goods exhibited, strategic placement of lovely, luxurious goods captured the eye and lured them inside.

The proprietors of Blakely's Shoppe were a pair of haughty sisters who had emigrated from Britain to Ontario. A tale was told that they had been very wealthy in England, but their family had lost everything. Thus, they settled in Canada because of the anonymity distance provided them.

The women were unmarried, had pale hair, fair skin, gray eyes and dressed alike. In the summer they wore lightweight black silk dresses, and when fall came, they switched to cashmere black wool sweaters and skirts. Pearls adorned their thin aristocratic necks and dainty watches their wrists. Their feet were housed in unattractive but sensible shoes.

Yearly, Mother would make it a point to go to this ritzy shop before returning to our Western New York home.

"No! No! No, I am not going with you to that snotty store," I exclaimed one year. I was a young teen now and extremely aware of what to expect there, yet I knew my objections were doomed to failure even as I loudly protested.

My sister Myrna had accompanied Mother in spring to check what she might want to purchase in September, so now it was my turn to suffer a visit to Blakely's. I joined her for this dreaded ordeal, albeit reluctantly.

The store, while not large, had a collection of beautiful pieces that catered to a discerning clientele. Most of their items were not for the average person and that included my mother. She could not have afforded the expensive fine Royal Albert dishes she so admired, the set of the delicate Waterford stemware, the classic Dalton figurines or Rosenthal collectors plate, but she could afford something far less grand. It was a fine bone china teacup imported from the British Isles. Thus far she had collected eight such treasures, all very distinct, all very lovely.

When Mother entered the store, the Blakely sisters' eyes narrowed as they judged her and found her lacking. She did not have the look of affluence most of their customers did. Their pale eyes did not disguise the distaste they felt at the effrontery she had in even stepping inside their elegant store.

Mother seemed oblivious to the haughty stares and nasty looks the sisters cast our way. To me, the animosity that emanated from them was palpable. I felt nauseous being in this uncomfortable atmosphere. Other people came in and were treated with courtesy, even fawned upon. We wandered about unattended as though invisible.

As usual, Mother took an interminably long time deciding which cup she wished to possess. She ambled back and forth between displays to determine which she yearned for most. "Come on. Choose already," I pleaded desperately. Her hand on her chin she pondered whether her choice should be the classic gold with a bouquet of gold mixed flowers in the middle of the teacup, or the unusual black lacy one adorned with a single red rose in its center. She seemed to be unaware of the owners' appallingly rude behavior. Absolutely nothing was going to keep her from leaving that shop with a well-deserved teacup for her labors at the Majestic.

Finally, she made a decision. We waited patiently at the counter until the proprietress came over to finalize the purchase. Miss

Blakely wrapped the gold cup in tissue and a white box, and Mother paid her in worn, colorful Canadian bills. She exited the Blakely's Shoppe, prize in hand, beaming.

"Why do you even go into that place?" I asked her. "Every time we go in there, they ignore you like you're not good enough for their snobby shop. It's disgraceful. You absolutely should not patronize them. They're a bunch of snobs and I find it humiliating."

Mother was smiling, oblivious to my complaints. "It's a very fancy store," she shrugged "and that's the way they are. I'm going to check the receipts and see if I can buy that black cup with the lace. It's called Señorita," she trilled. "I've never seen such an unusual teacup like that one."

I clamped my lips shut and said nothing more. My mother had been living in the United States for years, ran her cottage with an iron hand, and was generally considered formidable, yet here she was intimidated by Blakely's Shoppe. Possibly she equated ownership of something purchased there as a sign of gentility. It seemed to make her happier and prouder to own these elegant teacups from there than I could ever possibly imagine. To me they were simply cups. To her they were symbols of the more graceful life she strived for.

Over time, Mother managed to collect twenty of these delicate bone china cups. She proudly served tea in them for holidays, anniversaries, and birthdays, year after year. She set them upon glass shelves in the mahogany breakfront of our dining room, and most prominently displayed was always the unique teacup, Señorita, that Mother had rescued so many years ago from Blakely's.

Years passed and of all people, I inherited her collection when she passed away. The cups found a place in my china cupboard and as my mother before me, I too served hot beverages in them for special occasions. After they were used, I'd carefully hand wash and dry them before returning them to their home in the cupboard.

As time went by, I found other items I wanted to display on those shelves and stored the cups away in special storage containers that protected each piece in its own separate compartment. They were still easily available when I wanted to use them, and they were always a topic of conversation. I could say with confidence, "This was my mother's first cup. Oh, that one was a gift from my dad on their anniversary. Yes, the gold and white one is so unusual. Only a very limited amount of those were fired."

Now the entire collection has found a new nest. Today, these fragile cups are displayed in my daughter Julie's dining room. They rest on the wainscot trim that surrounds her dining hall walls; this small ledge no more than five inches wide now houses these delicate heirlooms. They seem to have found their rightful home. I find myself smiling when I listen to Julie explain in great detail the background of each cup as I did years before.

"Grandma bought this cup the day after they closed the cottage for the season and were already driving back to Buffalo. She hoped it hadn't been sold yet and luckily it was still there. It's called Señorita. Look at the delicate lace. Look at the rose in the center."

She chuckles, "I'm sure glad the Majestic had a really, really good summer that year."

23
Moving Out

By the last Sunday of August, the Majestic's season was winding down. By then everyone but us had packed up and left for their winter homes. A massive job of closing it up awaited us all. Dad had already begun by boarding up the vacant cabins in the back and Mother laundered linens as soon as people vacated their rooms. The last ten days before Labor Day were pretty quiet, so we were able to get a head start on what needed to be done.

All summer long, the Majestic was a noisy, breathing, messy animal that required our constant attention to keep it neat and operational. The grounds demanded care in mowing the grass, trimming the bushes, and watering the flowers. Around twilight, one of us would hose down all the backyard furniture and the patios in the back and front of the cottage so they would be clean for the next day's use. Inside, the Majestic needed its share of care, too. There was always something that needed to be washed, moved, mended, oiled, or replaced.

When all the guests left, we could finally relax mentally, but there was still plenty to do. To some, closing up the cottage might have suggested that all we had to do was turn the key in the lock and walk away. The grim reality was that my family was exhausted by the time that key actually wound up turning the lock on the Majestic.

The cottage had to be winterized from the outside in. My sisters and I lugged the Crayola colored steel chairs, wooden rockers and plastic tables onto a veranda already filled with wicker furniture. Together we rolled up the patio awning and the table umbrellas, then secured them with rope. The front porch was the only place these items could go to as we didn't have a shed or garage. The area became so congested that only a small path remained to get through to the outside door.

Dad rid the charcoal grills of ashes, scrubbed them clean with a wire brush, then found a nook for them in the laundry room along with drained garden hoses. Down came the flower pots. The soil returned to earth and the geraniums were unceremoniously tossed out. The fragile strings of outdoor lights were undone, and then rolled in tissue paper along with the delicate wind chimes. Stripped now of all its finery, the back yard looked just so ordinary, so drab.

Inside, Mother mopped down all the floors in the rental bedrooms and drew the window shades. They were now all officially shut down until next year. Myrna and I packed up our things for the trip home the next day.

We couldn't leave Crystal Beach without one last visit to the park. Mother headed for the Bingo Pavilion and Dad escorted us to the amusements. The *Buffalo Evening News* published coupons that were redeemable for additional tickets on rides when turned in at any Hall's Park ticket booth. Dad collected many of these coveted *News* strips from buddies at work, and we were excited to use them for our amusement rides this Labor Day weekend. The only hitch was that Dad insisted on coming with us.

"Hey Dad," I had argued, "I'm fourteen now and don't really need a nursemaid. I'll watch over Myrna."

"Don't worry," he smiled, "you won't even know I'm there. We won't talk. We won't walk together. I'll just be an extra pair of eyes."

"Myrna and I always come out to the park by ourselves. Why do you have to tag around with us tonight?"

Dad shook his head. "We just got here, and I think we'll be leaving close to midnight. I don't want you girls out that late alone. I'll pretend I don't even know you."

Myrna and I chose rides to go on and Dad set up a nearby meeting place for us to reconnect afterwards. We were always in the same vicinity. Dad took Linda on the Carousel, and Myrna and I rode the Hey Dey bumper cars, Caterpillar, and Splash, where we steered boats on the enclosed waterway. Dad and Linda waited to watch us when we went on something scary such as the Ferris wheel, the Comet roller coaster, or the Sky Ride, a small cart that shakily sailed over swaths of the park and Lake Erie at great heights. When we got off each ride, there he was waiting, a smile on his face.

When Dad took Linda into Kiddie Land, he insisted that Myrna and I come, too. Kiddie Land, located in the center of the park, had tame, miniature amusements for small children. Every time I complained about hanging around there, his answer was that this was a holiday weekend and people drank too much.

In little less than three hours, we had gone through all the tickets, eaten a late snack, and now walked through the grove to collect our mother from Bingo. It was inching toward midnight. Before we left the park, Dad stopped and bought a dozen of Hall's gourmet peanut and cinnamon suckers to take back to Buffalo with us when we left the next day.

Myrna and I walked toward home, and our parents trailed behind us. Dad was carrying a sleepy Linda back to the cottage. As Myrna and I passed the very crowded Cronfelt's Loganberry stand on Derby Street, a large man staggered away from the stand toward me.

"Hi, cutie," he said, and suddenly grabbed me about the waist. He kissed me on the mouth, and I could smell his beer breath. Instead of being afraid, I was angry and disgusted. Who on earth did he think he was? Without thinking, I brought my arm up and slapped him hard across the cheek.

"Hey, you little brat," he screamed, "that wasn't very nice." He grabbed my arm.

"What the heck is going on here?" Dad shouted, suddenly at my side.

"Sorry. Sorry," the man muttered and slithered away.

Once back at the cottage, I felt badly about how I had treated my father at the park and didn't know quite how to apologize.

Dad patted me on the shoulder. "Guess I was wrong. You *can* take care of yourself."

I threw myself into his arms. "Not all the time," I cried. "So glad you were with me. It ruined our last night here."

"Nah," he said. "Nothin' ruins our vacations here."

The next morning it was as if nothing had happened at all. There was no time to ruminate about yesterday. Rooms we were still using had to be cleaned up. Myrna and I scoured the pantry cupboards. After breakfast, all remaining unused food was scrapped and even more trash was taken out to the curb. Mother disconnected the refrigerator and left it open to air. She had prepared our lunch of sandwiches, fruit and sodas and packed it in a cooler for the trip home.

Myrna and I stripped the linens we had slept on the night before and threw them into plastic bags where they would be laundered in Buffalo. Dad padlocked the outdoor bathroom and laundry room doors. He shut off the water and drained the pipes. Mother conducted a final check, going slowly from room to room, sprinkling mothballs in the dressers, assuring herself that all was as it should be. The day after we left, the electricity would be turned off. Dad inserted the house key into the front door lock, securely turned it, and then we finally walked away.

At last, we were all packed up and settled in the car ready to drive home to Buffalo. For a moment everyone sat quietly studying the Majestic Cottage for the last time this year. It would probably be April before we came this way again.

Dad put the car in gear and slowly began to drive away. We all sighed.

The 'beast' that was the Majestic had once again been coaxed into hibernation.

24
Closing Of The Majestic

Labor Day was the last day of the Crystal Beach season. The park officially closed at midnight. Most people would leave the next day, not to return until the following year.

It was also the night of a distinctive ritual. Teenaged residents of the beach would dress in wild, flashy attire, and wear multi-colored beads about their necks, crowns of summer flowers around their heads for the annual local event called "Bury the Summer." A large cardboard box was transfigured into a makeshift coffin, adorned with bright strips of fabric, flowers, and ribbon streamers.

At twilight, the solemn procession began. Cars would slowly inch by, with mournful young people leading the way. Pallbearers held high the pseudo coffin surrounded by grief-stricken minstrels pounding out funereal dirges on their wailing harmonicas, slowly banging together tin pie plates, and shaking tambourines. As our destination neared, many of the girls dressed in flowing dresses broke away from the group to dance, looking like druids of old as they swayed and wove their way down to the shores of Lake Erie

Across the cold sand, we'd trudge to place the coffin down near the lake's edge with great ceremony. My friends and I would gather sticks and light bonfires here and there on the deserted beach. Amidst the acrid fumes, we'd wait until the night was black and the moon appeared. Somber words were uttered about the passing of the summer, while dramatic beachcombers threw themselves upon the coffin evincing great pain. Serenaded by a chorus of sorrowful farewells, the coffin was gently thrust out into the lake. We had no bow or lighted arrow to ignite the coffin, so we used a slender branch to set the cardboard casket afire.

As we watched the flames obliterate this last summer's memory, melancholy would descend. Too soon, our pagan Viking funeral concluded, and the lake became black again. The absolute unshakeable confidence that there would always be another summer to look forward to at the beach helped lessened our gloom. We danced about the fires, sad that summer at Crystal Beach had ended, yet happy we'd be back once again next year.

During the season, thousands of people had come to Crystal Beach daily on the *S.S Canadiana*, a steamship that ferried Americans from Buffalo to Canada. The lake trip took approximately seventy-five minutes to travel twenty-five gentle miles to Crystal Beach. It was powered by a coal-fired steam engine. The *Canadiana* boasted three wooden decks, promenades to wander about, and slot machines inside the main cabin to try your luck.

Boarding the *Canadiana* Steamship for a day at Crystal Beach was the beginning of an adventure, a voyage to Never, Neverland. The adventure didn't even end when one boarded the boat to head back to Buffalo. The ship was lit with thousands of lights, had a dance floor, and hosted bands that played popular music as one rode home on the waves.

Lamentably, the glory days of the *Canadiana* ended abruptly in 1958 when uncontrolled riots broke out on the ship. When the steamship suspended its crossings, it was a bad omen, but little did anyone know it was a harbinger of doom for the Mecca that was Crystal Beach.

The *Canadiana* had been the main mode of transportation for thousands of Buffalonians who made the journey daily. With the steamship's demise, the only choice left for Americans to get to the beach was either by car or bus, which meant driving on clogged, one-lane country roads and enduring long lines at immigration checkpoints.

The people who stayed at our cottage were mainly Canadians, so we were mostly unaffected by the cessation of the *Canadiana* sailings. As long as the amusement park stayed open, we could operate. After over a hundred years as a thriving summer attraction, Crystal Beach, however, was en route to an undignified demise. Many small restaurants and businesses simply couldn't survive the lessened attendance. Every year more local businesses shuttered, escalating the spiral to obscurity. Perhaps not every Viking funeral portends a rebirth of another glorious season.

In 1968, Dad retired, my parents sold their home in Buffalo and moved to Miami. They had expected to live in Florida during the winter months and spend their summers in Canada at the Majestic. Theoretically, it was the best of two worlds, but it soon proved to be an unrealistic goal.

That first year back at the cottage, they found themselves doing everything much more slowly. The drive back from Florida tired them out even before they got to the cottage. Although it wasn't something Dad was comfortable with, he hired a year-rounder to open up the cottage, trim the hedges, wash the windows, and do small repairs. Mother found two teenaged girls to come out regularly to help with the housework, especially the laundry. My sisters' lives and my own were in the States, so we rarely came out to visit except for weekends. Sometimes there wasn't even room for us to stay the night. The Majestic was still thriving, full of visitors.

Yet, there was no doubt it was becoming much more difficult for our parents to sustain their old standards. At the end of that first summer, return guests were told no reservations were going to be accepted for the following year. It was uncertain if the Majestic would reopen as our parents were exhausted by September.

That next spring, they did return, a bit later than usual, mid- May instead of April. It had become clear to them it was now time to sell the cottage. The Majestic was never open for business again. My oldest daughter Lori said that she felt the forthcoming closure of the Majestic most keenly. She and her sisters had cherished their days there, and soon it would no longer be theirs.

My parents lived there, just the two of them, in that vast amount of space, no longer going to the beach or to the park; all the upstairs bedrooms were closed off, as were the outdoor cabins. The picnic tables were not brought into the yard. There were no pots of geraniums arranged randomly, no outdoor chimes, no backyard canopy. Dad brought out a couple of porch chairs for them to sit out on the veranda. The day Dad climbed a ladder and removed the yellow Majestic sign from its perch, we knew things had changed forever.

The cottage sold quickly because it had been so lovingly cared for. Occupancy was Mom and Dad's until the middle of August. After all the many years of sharing their space with so many others it must have seemed strange to them to be all alone there, or perhaps they savored the peace. For eighteen years this cottage had been an integral part of their lives and now it was coming to an end. Their acceptance was absolute. If there was any regret about the sale, it wasn't evident. My sisters and I knew beyond any doubt that the time was right to let go of the beloved Majestic, but its passing seemed so unmourned.

Eventually, Hall's Amusement Park closed and that was Crystal Beach's death knell. The diamond-studded beachfront was reconfigured to accommodate luxury condos. The park became a gated community, residents driving golf carts over the expanse. The beach that had been a refuge for so many, was now off-limits to outsiders. Gentrification had arrived.

As the years passed, there was very little to enjoy at Crystal Beach. Bustling stores and restaurants had closed years ago. Many private cottages were simply left abandoned. The only portion of beachfront open to the public was a fenced off, minuscule strip of Bay Beach, unsupervised and sparsely attended. Despite all these changes, my sisters and I made pilgrimages to the cottage yearly although it was no longer ours. On one of the last occasions we went, my daughter Sue spotted the owners outside and asked if we could come in, after explaining our long years as owners.

As I entered the parlor, once again the elegant antique mirror greeted me. How incongruous was it that this magnificent piece still lived in a summer cottage? I was astonished at how crowded most of the bedrooms were, furnished with only a bed and chest of drawers. Where the regular Friday night poker games had been played sat only a sixty-inch round table. How on earth had all those men squeezed around it? The walls of the kitchen area were now painted pale lemon. I chuckled. Had it ever really been as orange as the inside of a cantaloupe? My glance fell to the old-fashioned stove, on which antiquated piece of equipment my sister had once baked a masterpiece.

As I passed through the cottage to the backyard, I could almost hear the rumblings of my mother's washing machine, smell the bacon sizzling on the grill, and hear the tinkle of the wind chimes. The backyard conjured up the bittersweet memories of Miz Delly and the camaraderie our tenants shared with us as we watched the embers from the barbecue fires crackle and die. Weeds had grown between the cracks of the outdoor patio. Once, long ago, a pale faced ballerina had floated in air lit mostly by moonlight.

As I left, still in the grip of these poignant memories, thinking of that simpler time, longing for one last glimpse of parents so long gone, I paused. My eyes caught sight of the black mezuzah, the religious symbol my dad had nailed to the frame of the front door to protect all who dwelled inside. Despite the passage of years and many different owners, it remained there still, firmly fixed in place, an undeniable reminder that once our family had called the Majestic home.

Unquestionably, we had left our mark.

Mom and Dad

My sister Myrna and I in front of the cottage

Eight years old, and noticing everything

Here I am standing above Mother and Father,
Linda in the middle

Made in the USA
Middletown, DE
09 April 2023

28294177R00109